The Promise of Tomorrow

Sandy Loyd

Editing by Pam Berehulke
www.BulletproofEditing.com

Cover Design by Kellie Ann Morgan
www.InspireCreativeServices.com

Dedication

Dear Reader:

At times I'm asked where I get the ideas for my books. Ideas can come from all sorts of places. This book is special because the idea came to me during the 2014 Kiss of Death Chapter's tour during RWA's National Conference. The chapter toured Lackland Air Base, where they train the Air Force's police force, and Fort Sam Houston, the Army's training center for field medics, where we were lucky enough to experience a simulated battle.

The story one medic told about having to watch his best friend die, helpless to do anything because his wounds were fatal, moved me to create a story that began with a character who had a similar experience. My goal is to spotlight the brave men and women at home and abroad who sacrifice much for our freedom.

This book is dedicated to all of those brave soldiers, their loved ones waiting back home, and especially to those who have lost loved ones or given their life or been injured for their country. You are all heroes and heroines in my mind.

Thank you and God bless.

Chapter 1

The sun peeked above the horizon, heralding another day. Just like the sixty-seven days before it, Corporal Roberto Camareno climbed out of his bunk at five thirty, ate his breakfast by six, and prepared himself for another monotonous day of patrolling.

He glanced at the cloudless sky through the tiny barracks window, trying to ignore a foreboding sense of doom that settled over his shoulders. As a medic, Cam was used to unsettling feelings, but this was different. He grabbed his gear, including his medical supplies, and let the screen door slam behind him.

What was so different about today? Shrugging, he kept walking and pushed the unease from his mind, a skill he'd perfected for survival.

Most likely it had something to do with it being Christmas Day.

Just another day in paradise, except this part of Afghanistan was more like hell on earth, considering the suffering he continually confronted. Cam had an admiration for the people who met such harsh conditions on a daily basis and still remained resilient enough to laugh and to find joy in the simplest of acts.

"Hey, Cam, wait up," Specialist Seth Baker called out.

Halfway to the Ground Mobility Vehicle, Cam halted and waited for his best friend to catch up.

"What'll it be today, my good man?" Seth held up his smartphone with a cord attached to a small speaker. Once turned on, it was barely loud enough to be heard over the GMV's engine noise. Still, it was better than nothing, and did much to ease the boredom of cruising the Afghan countryside looking for insurgents.

"A little bit of soul?" Seth waggled his eyebrows up and

down. "Or maybe some Christmas music to remind of us what day it is."

"Hell, Baker, this ain't a goddamned mall," Sergeant King said, emerging from the other side of the vehicle. "Keep that shit turned off."

"Aw, come on, Sarge. Where's your Christmas spirit?"

"Back in the States with my family," he shot back. "Which is where we all should be, rather than in this hellhole of a country." Sgt. Tahoe King never made any bones about his thoughts on being recalled to active duty, only to be redeployed a third time in a senseless war once his initial enlistment had ended.

Sergeant King heaved his backpack over one shoulder and his weapon over the other, muttering something about how Congress and the fricking crazies in Washington owned his ass for another three months. Like most enlistees, Cam included, who signed on for a three-year active-duty commitment, Sergeant King never imagined his government would demand his services when America was at peace. Then he said a little louder, "So, let's get moving. Once our mission for the day is accomplished, we can sit around and drink to Christ's birth while wishing we were home with our families."

"Aw, Sarge, aren't we your family?" Seth smiled amicably and placed an arm around his shoulder when Sergeant King flashed him a *not in this lifetime* look.

Cam laughed. Though forced to fight a cause he didn't agree with, Sergeant King, a demolitions expert, didn't shirk his duty. Besides being their squad leader, King trained Afghan soldiers about explosives in hopes they'd become adept at his expertise—both finding explosives and detonating them.

Following Sergeant King, they loaded into the vehicle and Private First Class Michael Sparks started her up. Once moving, Sparks veered to the far right side of the road, staying on a trail that had already been cleared.

The vehicle lurched and bounced on the dusty pitted road. Cam placed his hands under his butt in an effort to cushion it. He had enough bruises from being jostled over the past nine months to last a lifetime. Still, his lot was easy compared to the Afghans and their children, who could lose a limb or a life with one wrong step.

He glanced out at the rocky land that from this distance appeared to be an innocuous setting.

Terrorists had planted enough IEDs to blow up the entire countryside, which in turn incited more terror, death, and destruction. Cam and his friends would have been long dead if not for the man sitting next to him. No one had died on Sergeant King's watch, thanks to his keen eye and skill—a skill learned while living in the worst part of San Jose, as Sarge was fond of saying. Honing it aided in his surviving to adulthood.

Cam curled a hand, but uncurled it when there was no wood to knock on. Besides, Cam didn't rely on luck. Having come from a similar background as his sergeant's, he relied on what he'd learned on the streets.

Despite the order to stop with the Christmas music, they'd begun singing carols. After a moving rendition of "Silent Night," the melody faded away. Only the noise of the GMV's engine remained until Sparks's voice rang out. "Jingle bells. Jingle bells . . ." Within seconds, the others joined in. Even Sergeant King's scowl couldn't subdue the merriment of the moment.

A kid ran in front of the Humvee, and Sparks slammed on the brakes. The vehicle screeched to a stop, and everyone inside lurched forward.

As Cam anchored himself with a hand on the seat back, the engine died. Sparks hadn't engaged the clutch quickly enough.

The dust settled.

"Where the hell is he?" Sparks peered out his window. The kid was nowhere to be seen. "I know I didn't hit him."

Everything was too quiet. The hairs on the back of Cam's neck stood on end.

"Let's check it out." Tahoe reached for the door latch.

Suddenly the world exploded in one loud bang.

At rocket-launch speed, Cam flew out of the Humvee.

He landed hard. His ears rang as he struggled to sit up. Every muscle in his body hurt. An acrid smell of burning rubber hit his nostrils. When the smoke cleared, he took in the carnage around him.

Sparks had a hand to his forehead to staunch the flow of blood running into his face. A swatch of hair was missing from his scalp. Private First Class McVey, another soldier who'd been sitting beside Cam, was bleeding from an obvious leg wound.

"You've been injured," Cam said to McVey, then grabbed his bag and rolled next to him. "I've got to stop the bleeding."

McVey looked down at his blood-drenched pant leg. Then his gaze focused on Cam's shoulder. "You're bleeding too."

"Shit." Cam hadn't even noticed his arm had taken on shrapnel. He had to act fast to contain the bleeding. A soldier was more likely to lose his life due to blood loss rather than his injuries.

McVey helped him wrap a bandage strip around his wound. Once done, Cam ripped the strip and tied it as tight as he could.

Moving swiftly, he cut away McVey's pant leg, then cleaned and bandaged the three-inch gash on his leg. The coppery scent of blood usually didn't bother him, but now he gagged at the smell surrounding him.

"What about Seth?" McVey pointed a few feet away.

That was when Cam first noticed Seth. He ignored the fire in his upper arm. Nothing hurt as bad as seeing his friend's crumpled body just a few feet away. Blood soaked Seth's chest, face, and arms.

McVey made eye contact with him and hobbled to Seth's bleeding body. He knelt at Seth's side and lifted what was left of his bloody shirt off his chest before meeting Cam's gaze again. "Shit," he whispered. "You gotta help him."

Wiping the moisture out of his eyes with the back of his hand, Cam shot back, "Triage, man, I gotta save the living first." His job was assessing the likelihood of survival and treating those who'd live with his efforts until help arrived. Even from this distance, it was clear Seth's wounds were fatal.

"Can't you do anything?" The emotion in McVey's question wasn't helping Cam's resolve to stick to procedure.

"Yeah. I can bandage Sparks's head and pray he doesn't bleed out before help gets here."

Sometimes his job sucked. He pulled more bandages out of his bag and added as he washed away some of the dirt and debris, "In the meantime, maybe you can staunch the flow of blood from Baker's stomach wounds until I finish with Sarge and Tucker." His nod indicated the other two men facedown in the dirt, the dusty ground turning a dark red under them. "That's all that can be done for him at this point."

Cam cleared his throat and blinked, trying to focus on saving the men he could. It hurt to have to make the determination that his friend's wounds were too extensive for survival. What if he were wrong? A quick look back at Seth didn't disabuse his conviction, nor did it do much to assuage his doubts.

"Chopper's on the way." The distinct sound of the slicing blades eased Cam's mind as he completed bandaging Sparks's head. He grabbed his bag and ran to the other two soldiers.

Sergeant King's right leg was gone below the knee. Cam worked quickly to stop the bleeding. Tucker's wounds weren't as serious. Behind him, a chopper landed and men with stretchers exited, running toward the casualties.

"Shit, what the hell happened?" Sergeant King asked groggily as he came to once he was laid on the stretcher.

"The kid was wired is my guess," Tucker said as Cam ran back to McVey and Seth. That was when he noticed the unrecognizable bloody mess beside what was left of the GMV.

"Who would wire a kid?" Though whispered, Sarge's tone left no doubt that the idea angered him. "And on Christmas Day?"

Terrorists who wanted to strike at the heart of good and decent human beings, that's who. That thought, along with the need to save his buddy, ran through Cam's consciousness as he knelt next to Seth. Using one of the towels McVey had given him, he pressed it to what was left of Seth's chest.

"What a way to go," Seth croaked as the medical technician placed him on a stretcher.

Blinking back tears, Cam remained next to his friend until he was loaded onto the chopper. "Can I sit next to him?"

"Yeah," the medic said, "but you're not lookin' so good

yourself."

Cam waved off the medic's concern. He should be the one dying, not his friend who had a fiancée at home waiting for his return.

"Hey, buddy, looks like this is it for me."

Seth's raspy voice drew Cam's gaze. "You can't give up. You're engaged to be married."

His friend offered a semblance of a smile. "That's what I want to talk to you about." He coughed up blood.

"Easy, man," Cam murmured, dabbing at the red droplets running down his chin.

"No." Seth struggled to sit up, but the effort cost him and he dropped back down. "You gotta promise me you'll look after her and make sure she's okay."

Cam knew Seth was talking about his fiancée. They would have been married by now if their unit hadn't deployed. Seth didn't want to marry and then have to leave a few weeks later, so they postponed their wedding. Cam was going to be his best man. He'd never met Nicole Murphy, but after listening to Seth sing her praises for six months, he figured he'd know her on sight. Yet he never expected it to be at a funeral rather than a wedding.

"You're gonna make it. I don't want you to die," Cam said in a choked voice.

"I prefer living." Seth's voice was barely audible as he clasped Cam's hand. "But we both know it ain't gonna happen. So promise me you'll take care of her."

Cam closed his eyes, wishing with all his might he could change places with his friend.

Why, Lord? Why?

That was one question he'd probably never have answered. A tear rolled down his face, and he didn't bother wiping it away as he nodded. "Yeah, man. Of course I'll take care of her. You don't have to worry. Just try to stay alive."

"I love you." Seth released the hold on his hand, closed his eyes, and sighed with relief. "You're a good man."

"I love you too, good buddy," Cam whispered.

Seconds later, Seth's body went slack.
At that point Cam couldn't hold back the tears.
If only he could have done something to save him.

Chapter 2

Eleven months later

Cam left the station as soon as his EMT shift ended. Horns and traffic noise blared around him as he walked the few blocks to his apartment. A light drizzle dampened his hair. Shivering, he snapped his windbreaker all the way up and shoved his hands into his pockets to ward off the chill from the brisk breeze that seemed to cut right through him.

It was times like this he wished he hadn't sold his car before he left for Afghanistan.

In the eight months he'd been back in California, his lack of transportation hadn't been a problem. In fact he usually enjoyed his walks, especially when his shift ended after midnight and the streets were quiet—if he avoided certain areas. Cam's apartment skirted one of the roughest and poorest neighborhoods in San Jose.

Yet tonight the walk was anything but enjoyable, and the rain had nothing to do with his morose mood. Everywhere he looked, green and red permeated the landscape. It was the season when Thanksgiving turkeys gave way to holiday lights. Christmas was fast approaching, a solid reminder of the upcoming anniversary of the worst day of his life.

His pace increased in an effort to outrun the memories. Unfortunately, it never worked. At his destination and not wanting to be a downer for the rest of the night, Cam pushed the thought away as he'd done a million times since his return, automatically retrieved his mail from the box, and climbed the stairs to his apartment.

It took only minutes to change out of his uniform and into

more comfortable jeans and a T-shirt that gave him the cloak of anonymity he preferred. Passersby on the street always reacted to the uniform—the same undeserved reaction of respect and admiration he received when wearing his Army uniform.

While eating a quick ham and cheese sandwich, he glanced through his mail, tossed the junk into the recycle bin, and opened the most pressing bill from his mother's assisted-living facility. Sighing, he stuck it, along with the tuition-due notice for the next semester of college, on his makeshift desk to pay later.

Cam gulped a glass of milk and polished off the last bite of his dinner before grabbing his jacket and heading back out the door. Studying for upcoming finals would have to wait until later that night.

At least the rain had stopped, he thought, walking toward the rehabilitation center where he volunteered two nights a week. Serving at the center eased the survivor guilt that continually consumed him. Most of those he came into contact with at the facility were ex-soldiers wounded in either Iraq or Afghanistan.

His injury had required arthroscopic surgery, which included a long and painful healing process. Yet he'd been lucky to regain one hundred percent use of his arm and shoulder. His ordeal had been nothing compared to guys he now helped at the center.

After signing in, he started for the gym.

"Well, I'll be. If it isn't Roberto Camareno."

Recognizing the familiar voice, Cam stopped and spun around. He squinted, not believing his eyes. "Tahoe? Is that you?"

"In the flesh!" Wearing a huge smile, Tahoe King held out a hand. "How the hell are you, man?" A raspy laugh followed. "Tried to look you up, but it's like you fell off the face of the earth."

A flush of heat hit Cam's cheeks, and he could barely make eye contact with his fellow comrade in arms. "After rehab, time had a way of slipping by."

It shamed him to admit to losing touch with the guys who'd ridden with him on that fateful day nearly a year ago. Worse, he'd never made an attempt to contact any of them. Didn't matter that his lack of communication was due more to guilt than lack of caring. Nor did it make him feel any less like an ass for not at least following up with a call or a card.

"'Course," Tahoe went on, either unaware of Cam's discomfort or choosing to ignore it, "I'm not as whole as I used to be, but with technology, I'm pretty damned close."

That was when Cam noticed the curved blade below Tahoe's knee. He swallowed hard. Memories he'd fought to subdue came at him fast and furious, as if the explosion that changed all their lives had happened an hour ago rather than almost a year.

"I'm sorry about your leg, Sarge."

Tahoe waved the sentiment off. "Me too, but I can't change anything so I chose to overcome it instead." He lifted the leg, showing the blade attached to his knee at a better angle, and patted his thigh. "It's why I'm here. I'm a bright example of life after losing a limb."

To prove his point he did a good imitation of a boxer, taking fake punches as he danced around. Tahoe slowed his steps, his curious gaze landing on Cam's face. "So, what brings you here?"

"Same as you. Helping out where I can." He ran a hand through his hair and stared at a spot on the floor. Except he was a fraud, definitely not an example to follow. Hell, he couldn't even bring himself to look up Seth's fiancée in the flesh. How did one go about doing that anyway?

To give himself some credit, he had found her on the Internet. Seth's Nicole lived half an hour east of him, but it might as well have been thirty hours because he'd never gotten up the nerve to try to meet her. He found snippets of information about her on Facebook and followed her on Twitter. Doing both had been enough to convince himself that she was fine. Nicole Murphy had a truckload of family and friends. A woman that lucky damn sure didn't need him and his baggage mucking up her life.

"After we're done, we should grab a drink and catch up."

Tahoe's enthusiastic voice drew him out of his thoughts, and he looked up.

"And now that we've reconnected, we should stay in better

touch." Tahoe pulled out his cell phone and glanced questioningly at Cam. They exchanged numbers before his friend tucked his phone back in his pocket, then turned to leave. "See you in a few hours."

Cam nodded and kept his gaze fastened on Tahoe until he disappeared through the double doors at the end of the hallway. Since it was best not to dwell on his deficiencies, he planned to bury himself in working extra hard with the men who needed his help.

He stayed busy enough over the next two hours to keep the memories at bay. When it was time to leave, he searched for Tahoe and found him with a patient. Not wanting to interrupt, he felt only relief as he quietly did a one-eighty and headed for the exit, not that he was trying to escape.

"Hey, wait up." Tahoe's voice stopped Cam in his tracks as the door swung open into the night. "Thought we were going for drinks."

Hands in his pockets, Cam turned around, struggling to present a careless smile. "You were involved with a patient, and I was done for the night. Besides, I have finals to study for. I figured we could go for a beer another time."

"You in school?"

When Cam nodded, a huge grin broke out on Tahoe's face. "So am I, man. Come on, forget the beer. The least you can do is spare a few minutes and buy me a cup of coffee."

Having no choice, he fell into step beside his friend.

"I was hoping you had a car," Tahoe said, his voice breaking the silence.

Shaking his head, Cam quickly explained about selling his car and banking the proceeds. "Good thing too, since I needed money for an apartment when I got back from Afghanistan." San Jose was an expensive city. As an EMT, he earned a decent salary, but funds only stretched so far when part of it provided for an aging mother with severe arthritis. Anything left over went to his classes. "I plan to get a car when I graduate."

Tahoe snorted. "Yeah, I hear ya. Not being able to drive is the hardest part of having only one good foot—a left one at that.

I'm saving for one of those cars with hand controls, but . . ." He shrugged. "Like you, money's tight."

Tahoe sighed, then asked after brief pause, "So, how'd you get out of active duty?"

Where did he start? Cam's best option was to offer the truth. "After recovering from shoulder surgery, I had the choice of going back to the old unit or going home."

He hesitated until Tahoe said, "And?"

"I chose to go home." He peered down at the ground. "The people I loved were no longer there." He left out the part about missing Seth's memorial service at Arlington. Tahoe wouldn't understand his motives. Hell, he didn't understand them. He just knew he hadn't been able to deal with the situation, so he'd ignored it.

"And you've been here all this time?" There was no accusation in Tahoe's question, only curiosity.

By now, they'd reached The Caffeine Zone. Thankful for the timely distraction, Cam held the door open.

"So, what are you majoring in?" Tahoe asked after the waitress had taken their orders.

Relieved to have the conversation back to neutral ground, Cam set the menu in its slot. "I'm studying to be a physical therapist." His goal was something he was comfortable with sharing.

"Is that because of what happened to us?"

A lump formed in the back of Cam's throat. He nodded, then cleared his throat, and finally was able to croak out, "What about you?"

"I'm working toward my BS in Marketing, using the GI Bill. Hopefully, once I graduate, I can work someplace that has tuition assistance. My long-term goal is to go for my MBA."

"That sounds like a great plan." He was taking advantage of the new GI Bill too.

"Yeah, well, I need to support a family. Not having two legs makes it tough to go back to my old job on the docks in Oakland. You know—before Uncle Sam called me back to active duty." He snorted. "There's not a lot of opportunities for a demolitions expert in East San Jose—unless you're in a gang." His gaze roamed to the waitress heading their way. "I'm doing my best to keep on top of school."

"College is tough." Cam's year wasn't going as smoothly as he'd hoped. Thankfully, he'd gotten most of his core content out of the way in the classes the military offered online. "Do you feel old? Like you're with a bunch of kids?" He certainly did.

"Hell yes. I *am* old." Tahoe waited for the waitress to set two steaming cups of coffee in front of them. As she left, he placed his hands around the mug as if warming them. "I don't have anything in common with most of the students in my classes."

"I hear ya," Cam murmured in agreement.

"For one thing, I have a wife and two kids to consider." Tahoe brought the coffee to his lips and took a sip. "None of those frat boys spending Daddy's money think they'll ever be married."

"Those guys seem too immature to ever be a father." Other than his mom, Cam didn't have a family, but he didn't have much in common with his classmates either. Too many were there to drink and screw. He'd left the partying behind when Seth died.

"I'm thankful they're around. They bring down the curve." Tahoe grinned. "I'm just as thankful most of the big brains are into engineering or medicine, rather than business. Those types negate the effects of the curve."

"I know the ones you mean." Yet he couldn't connect with them either; the work came easily to them. Not so for Cam. Chemistry and biology were tough subjects. "Hopefully, a three-point average will be enough to land a job at a rehab hospital." He had done the research and figured that with the baby boomers aging, PTs would be more in demand as time went on. It was a win-win in his mind.

They talked about their classes and their futures.

Finally, Cam looked at his watch and swore under his breath. He was enjoying Tahoe's company and hadn't paid attention to the time. "It's been great catching up, and we should do this again soon." He sincerely wished they could shoot the breeze longer. "But I really do have to study. I have two finals in the

13

morning and need to get at least an eighty percent on both to keep my B average." Cam's neighbor, a brainiac, was tutoring him, but even with that, he worked his tail off to get Bs.

"Yeah, me too." Tahoe rose. "Great seeing you."

Cam put down enough money to cover the bill and the tip.

Out on the street, the drizzling rain had resumed. With the wind, the mist might as well be barbs of ice the way they pierced his face and neck.

Cam's pace increased, as did Tahoe's.

"Are you still taking care of Seth's fiancée?"

"What?" Unsure that he heard correctly, his gaze flew to Tahoe's, and Cam's eyebrows shot up.

Tahoe offered a sheepish grin. "Like you promised Seth before he died. I caught the exchange and was just wondering."

"Oh . . . well . . ." Cam shrugged. "It's still on my to-do list."

"I see." Tahoe nodded and clenched his jaw, drawing his eyebrows together. "Don't wait too long."

Cam laughed, but there was no humor in the sound, only derision. Aimed at himself. "I hear you. I already feel like the scum of the earth for procrastinating." And wasn't that a bald-faced lie that came out too easily? Not about the scum part. Procrastination wasn't the real reason he'd never checked up on Seth's fiancée. Cam hadn't had the courage to meet her. The sudden realization did nothing to ease his guilt. Yet, what would he say? *I let your fiancé die?* No.

When Cam was about to turn the corner, Tahoe stopped. "I go this way." He held out his hand. "Remember, don't be a stranger."

After shaking hands, his ex-sergeant walked away. Cam watched him until he was out of sight, then headed in the opposite direction toward his apartment. One thought pervaded his mind—his promise to look after Seth's fiancée—or more accurately, his avoidance of doing so.

• • •

The acrid smell of sulfur mixed with the coppery scent of blood woke Cam from a deep sleep.

Seth stood at the bottom of his bed, holding his midsection with a bloody hand in an effort to keep his internal organs in place. "Buddy, you've let me down."

"What the hell." Cam bolted upright. Wide-eyed, he could only stare, too shocked to do much else. This couldn't be real.

When their gazes locked, accusation shone from Seth's eyes. "First you don't save me, and then you don't honor your promise to me."

Cam wiped the sleep out of his eyes and swallowed hard. Guilty on both counts, he thought. "I'm sorry," he whispered. What else could he say? That he'd been too busy to go and visit Nicole? "I friended her on Facebook and follow her on Twitter."

Shaking his head, Seth offered a sad, all-knowing smile that didn't ease Cam's guilt.

"She seems to be doing great." Once out, his comment sounded like a lame excuse, even to himself, but it was the truth. He had to make Seth understand. "Why bring back bad memories at this point?"

"Nicole needs you."

"No. She doesn't need me. I'll only weigh her down with my baggage."

"Honor your promise."

"I wish I could've taken your place, man." Cam blinked to clear moisture from his eyes. "You were the best friend I ever had."

"Honor your promise."

"How can I when it should have been me who died, not you?"

"Honor your promise."

"You don't understand." Tears streamed down his face. "I can't. I can't." He sat up in bed. The spot where Seth had stood was now empty.

"Damn," he whispered. It had been a *dream*. His apparition had been nothing but a dream. Or more accurately, a nightmare.

His guilty conscience was rearing its ugly head. He grabbed the pillow and pounded it before wrapping an arm around it and dropping back onto the bed. Lying there, he couldn't stop the

15

flood of memories seeping into his soul and keeping him awake.

The dreams were coming more often. Tonight's had seemed too real. If Cam didn't know better, he'd think Seth was haunting him.

No.

What haunted him was his lack of courage for not following through on the one thing Seth had asked him to do.

Cam would have to make good on his promise. And soon. If he didn't, his conscience would continue to haunt him in his dreams, just as it dogged his days.

Having come to that decision, he switched his thoughts to coming up with a plan. How hard could it be? Just go in and see her. Yeah, that would work. It had to work. He'd get right on it.

Sporting a grim smile, he punched the pillow one more time and closed his eyes.

Once he was convinced her life was on track, then he'd be square with his promise.

Chapter 3

"You have excellent taste, Mrs. Jones." Nicole Murphy placed the jewelry on the velvet pad. The sterling silver and cubic zirconia necklace shone brighter on the black background.

"Oh, how lovely. This will definitely perk up the gown I'm wearing for the Disabled Veteran's Gala Event." Mrs. Jones gave Nicole a pointed look. "You are going, aren't you?"

"Yes. She's going if I have to hog-tie her to my side," Mary Ann Davidson said, stepping into view and obviously overhearing their conversation.

Nicole squeezed out a smile at the same time sending Mary Ann a *butt-out* warning with her eyes. "I'm thinking about it."

Her older sister tended to overstep her bounds. A lot. Not that Nicole didn't feel blessed to have such a caring sister, but sometimes family could be a burden when one wanted to grieve in private.

"It's for an excellent cause, you know," Mrs. Jones added in a conspiratorial tone. "The theme is 'A Healing Christmas.'"

"I'm a huge supporter of your charity. In fact, I've already bought a ticket." Nicole shrugged. "I'm not sure I'll go, though."

"Oh, come on. You'll have fun." Rolling her eyes, Mary Ann placed her hands on her hips. "You'll be with us."

Yeah, as a third wheel. Rather than speak the thought out loud, Nicole nodded and kept her smile frozen in place. They meant well, but none of them could understand her feelings. This time of year no longer held any joy. Not after burying her fiancé almost a year ago. And seeing as how Seth died on Christmas Day, her feelings about celebrating the season weren't destined to change for a long while.

"Let me show you an awesome pair of earrings that would go

perfectly with this necklace," she said to steer the conversation away from the upcoming gala event. There was nothing healing about Christmas; the holidays were simply days to get through without falling apart. Nicole moved to another showcase. She spent a long moment unlocking the case and gathering the two pieces. "You should try them on."

"You are a tricky salesperson," Mrs. Jones said, clucking and reaching for the earrings. The older woman's grin negated the comment.

Mission accomplished, Nicole thought. The preferential treatment customers received when shopping was one of the main draws for women who came into Unlimited Accessories, and the lady now inserting an earring into her earlobe was no different. Though pricey, the costume jewelry Mary Ann created was eclectic and unlike anything the chain stores offered. Her sister also supplied hot cocoa and the best éclairs this side of the Sierras, along with a place to chat. Most of their customers were repeat buyers like Mrs. Jones, who spent at least an hour deciding on an item. Thank God, Mary Ann had plenty to choose from.

"They bring out my eyes." Mrs. Jones glanced in the mirror. Turning her head one way and then the other, she heaved a contented sigh. "They are perfect." She gave her head a slight shake and the earrings danced.

Nicole nodded. They did bring out the blue in the older woman's faded eyes. The earrings took twenty years off her face, even though deep wrinkles etched each side.

"Mary Ann, you are a genius." Mrs. Jones reached into her pocketbook. She turned to Nicole. "And you, young lady, certainly guessed my weak spot."

"Weak spot, my ass." Mary Ann snorted. "It's not a crime to spend a little money on yourself," she added in a huffy tone. "You know, besides putting it all toward your charities or your animals." Mrs. Jones was a widow who never had children, but she had two cats. Both cats wore jeweled collars that Mary Ann had created on consignment.

"After all, I know your secret." Mary Ann laughed.

Nicole grinned. So did she. One of her favorite charities was the organization presenting the gala. The disabled veteran's group ran a secondhand store where Nicole spent her spare time volunteering. Quite a few of the donated pieces being sold there were from Unlimited Accessories. Mrs. Jones was the donor.

It worked out because Mary Ann offered a hefty discount on the pieces, knowing where they would eventually end up. So indirectly, they were all giving to a good cause. Still, the woman was overly generous, in Nicole's opinion.

"I feel guilty that you give away so much of the jewelry you buy here." Nicole took an earring box and a necklace box out of the drawer. "You should save some for yourself like Mary Ann suggested."

"You make a strong argument. What if I tell you that I plan to wear them on Saturday night?"

"And knowing you, you'll be donating them to the silent auction," Mary Ann chimed in as Nicole followed the two women to the counter to ring up the sale. Sighing, her sister scolded, "I've already donated ten pieces."

"If it will make you happier, I'll refrain from adding these to the auction." Mrs. Jones glanced in the mirror next to the register. "I do think I love how these make my eyes sparkle. It would be a shame to give them away."

Nicole handed Mrs. Jones her receipt, along with the bag containing the jewelry boxes. "Here you are. You're all set to go."

"Thank you." The older lady turned toward the door and said over her shoulder, "Remember, I expect to see you both on Saturday night."

Mary Ann nodded. "You will." Then she glanced at Nicole and wrapped an arm around her. "Since it's benefiting wounded soldiers." She added a squeeze. "We wouldn't miss it. Right, sis?"

"Miss what?"

Nicole groaned as their mother, Colleen Murphy, came into view from the back of the shop. Colleen's best friend, Maggie McAllister, wasn't far behind.

Just what she needed. More arm twisting.

"The charity gala event that Mrs. J is co-chairing." Mary Ann let go and busied herself with a display she'd started working on before Mrs. Jones had entered the store.

"Of course you're going." Colleen frowned. "It's been almost a year since Seth died. You have to start living again. He wouldn't want you to grieve your youth away."

"It doesn't change what day he died. Christmas will never be the same again." Nicole's belly coiled into a tight knot. There was no possible way to escape attending the event. Somehow, she'd get through the night. Her mom was right about one thing. Seth wouldn't want to see her grieving her life away after his death. Besides, it was for a worthy cause. She only had to remember that.

"I know it's tough. Especially the first year." Colleen pulled her into a hug. "It'll get easier as time goes on."

Nicole nodded slowly, offering a slight smile. Easy for her mom to say when she wasn't the survivor who'd had her happily-ever-after crushed in one phone call.

Despite the warmth of her mother's arms surrounding her, Nicole still felt cold inside. Or numb was a better description.

Any and all dreams of marrying her own Prince Charming had faded after receiving the sketchy details of Seth's death. Nicole had already feared the worst when Seth hadn't e-mailed her on that fateful day. When his mother finally did relay the news a few days later, the older woman could barely talk. Having never been close, Nicole hadn't had the heart to ask for specifics. Now she rarely saw the Bakers. It was as if that phone call had severed her link to them.

Seth had been her entire world, and now he wasn't. Everyone expected her to move on. After all, she had only been a fiancée, not a widow, as too many people had reminded her. That fact hadn't stopped her heart from breaking. Nor did it do much to help it heal. She doubted it could heal considering the pain of loss that still pierced her heart.

As her mom let go, Nicole glanced at the clock on the wall. Thank God it was time for lunch. She moved to grab her purse. "I have errands to run." Then in an effort to appease the three women looking at her with compassion, she added, struggling to sound enthusiastic, "I have to shop for something to wear if I'm going to look presentable on Saturday night."

"That's the spirit," Maggie shouted as Nicole hurried out the front door.

• • •

The second the door closed behind Nicole's departing back, Colleen caught Mary Ann's gaze. "We have to do something."

"Mom." Mary Ann sent her a warning glare. "Stay out of it."

Of course her daughter would say that when she didn't understand the magnitude of the problem. "We can't just sit around and watch her close herself off to life." She looked to Maggie for support. "She's too young to be so uninterested in the opposite sex."

Maggie nodded. "Colleen's right."

"She buried her fiancé last year." Mary Ann huffed out an impatient sigh. "People don't grieve on your schedule."

"This is more than just grief. Besides, it wasn't like they were married, and Seth was gone for six months before he died." Colleen went behind the counter, busying herself with signing in to the sales register to begin her two-hour shift. "She's using his death as a reason to hide from life."

"Exactly." Maggie reached for a bottle of window cleaner behind the counter. "At this rate, she'll never recover." She sprayed and attacked the detested fingerprints customers left on the glass. "Not if she refuses to go out and have fun."

Done with one, Maggie moved to another showcase. "She needs to get back up on the dating horse, so to speak."

"You should let Nicole manage her loss in her own way." Shaking her head, Mary Ann grabbed her purse. "But I haven't got time to argue. I have an errand to run. Kyle's stepmom is down with the flu, so I'm taking her a care package. Thanks for coming in today." On her way out, she added over her shoulder, "I really appreciate the help."

"No problem," Colleen murmured, watching her daughter practically run out the exit. Finished with her task, she rummaged through a couple of drawers, searching for festive green and red ribbons, then began working on a Christmas display. The gaudier, the better at this time of year was her motto—although Mary Ann usually scaled down her efforts, claiming her jewelry was too high end to be treated like baubles at a discount store.

When done, she glanced at Maggie. "What do you think?"

"You definitely have a knack for merchandising." Maggie's grin was infectious. "I already bought a pair of those earrings. Just looking at that display makes me want to add the necklace."

"Go ahead and splurge."

Maggie laughed. "I need to get my Christmas shopping done before I buy any more presents for myself."

Colleen nodded and started on another case. "I love creating themed presentations." She pulled out a necklace, then reached for a neck rounder that would show off the design. "I'm happy Mary Ann asked us to work during the season." Her daughter had needed lunchtime help, and Colleen had needed something to keep her from going stark raving mad now that Nicole, her baby, had recently moved into her own studio apartment.

"So am I. Gets me out of the house." Maggie placed the cleaner under the counter before picking up the bracelet that went with the necklace. "Plus, it's an enjoyable two hours and seldom feels like work." She handed it to Colleen, who set it in the case.

"I'm not cut out to be an empty nester." She stood back to admire her handiwork, and then looked at Maggie to gauge her reaction.

Except Maggie wasn't paying any attention; she was staring out the plate-glass window instead. Finally, she sighed and turned her focus on Colleen. "What are we going to do about Nicole?"

"Good question." Colleen had pondered that same topic since Nicole had taken a leave of absence from teaching kindergarten last September. And she still had no answers. "Before Seth died, she was always busy doing fun things with her friends, along with her causes."

"It's unhealthy to whittle away every spare moment by volunteering like an old lady." Maggie clucked her tongue, and Colleen nodded in agreement.

When Nicole wasn't working at Unlimited Accessories, she

was working at the secondhand store. Where most people put in forty to sixty hours a week, she put in eighty. Her life revolved around work. All work and no play made for a dull person. And *dull* had never been a word to describe Nicole until after Seth's death.

"Maybe I should back off like Mary Ann suggests, but somehow I believe my youngest needs a push to get back to her old self." Colleen frowned. The thought of Nicole being all alone at night saddened her. Colleen was pretty sure the reason she moved into that studio apartment was so that no one would interfere with her withdrawal from life. "She dated so many boys in high school, I thought she'd never settle down. Yet from the moment she met Seth during her senior year, that was it." The memory brought a smile to her face. "Nicole always talked about having lots of children."

Her smile died and her throat grew tight. "Now she says she's never getting married." A pang pierced her heart at the thought. Despite being the youngest of Colleen's brood of nine, Nicole had been the first to announce her engagement. "I never thought I'd have to worry about her future or finding someone to share it with, but now that's all I do."

Colleen cleared her throat. "I understand the fierce bond of a first love." After all, she'd met her husband during her sophomore year, and they'd been together close to thirty-five years.

Maggie gave her a hug. "Don't worry. We'll think of something."

A customer stepped into the shop, interrupting her reply and walking briskly toward her. "I need a gift for my daughter-in-law. Something elegant."

Colleen smiled at the attractive, well-dressed woman and showed her to a case with Mary Ann's latest designs. But as she pulled out several pieces for the lady to try on, her thoughts were working on a way to help ease her daughter's pain.

Chapter 4

Cam hopped on BART and had his pick of seats. Afternoon rush hour for the city's transit system hadn't yet begun, so the car was half-empty. Thankfully, his finals were a done deal. He wasn't due at the station until early evening, and had plenty of time to take care of what he'd dubbed "the Nicole Murphy business."

At his stop, he hopped off and took the escalator stairs two at a time. Near the exit, a lone man sat holding up a sign. Cam dropped all his spare change into the panhandler's cup.

The quick smile he received in response revealed a couple of missing teeth. "Thanks, man."

"Don't mention it." Cam nodded and met his gaze for an instant before continuing on. In all likelihood, the guy was a vet who might well use the money for a drink. Cam understood all too well the need to anesthetize oneself from painful memories. There just wasn't enough care available to help the mental anguish that fighting in places like the Middle East or Southeast Asia caused.

He was one of the lucky ones whose reasons to fight to remain sane—his mom and a vow to never end up like his dad—actually worked. Maybe if his dad hadn't been a drunk and if his mom didn't need him, he might be sitting there beside the guy, sporting stringy hair and a long beard, with no idea of when his last shower was or whether he'd spend the night in a bed, under some cardboard box, or maybe in the damp, cold underground BART station.

Rubbing his hands together to warm them, Cam started walking, glad to be outside in the sunshine. Christmas was only two weeks away, yet the usual drizzly weather had drifted east. It was a gorgeous day. Last night's rain had cleared the air. At the end of the street, he took in a cleansing breath and glanced around to get his bearings.

According to Google Maps, the shop where Nicole Murphy worked was only a few blocks from the Hayward station.

The sun felt good on his face as he ventured forth. One thing he loved about living in the San Francisco Bay area—especially San Jose—was that it was nice ninety percent of the time. Summers never got too hot and winters never got too cold. During his tour in Afghanistan, he'd missed the hustle and bustle of the city. Everything was so different over in the Middle East. Customs were different. Women were treated differently. He'd been treated differently. Now he could just be anonymous. A man in a crowd. A man in a crowd with a mission he'd been too chicken to take care of until today.

The sign above the storefront read UNLIMITED ACCESSORIES, so he knew he was at the right place. He entered the store and saw an older woman who looked familiar.

"Can I help you?" One brow rose as she gave him a discreet once-over.

"I'm looking for Nicole Murphy." Cam stood taller. "I was told she works here."

The lady's eyes narrowed into suspicious slits. "And why might you be looking for my daughter?"

Cam smiled. Of course, that was why she looked familiar. He held out his hand. "Then you must be Mrs. Murphy. I'm Roberto Camareno."

"Nice to meet you Roberto, but please call me Colleen. When I hear someone say Mrs. Murphy, I always turn around and expect to see my mother-in-law." She shook his hand with a firm grip, even as her eyebrows arched once more. "Have we met?"

"Colleen it is, then." He liked her on the spot. "My friends call me Cam." Then to answer the question that still lurked in her eyes, he added, "No, we haven't met. I was in Seth's unit." He cleared his throat to ease the lump that suddenly formed. The lump grew, but he was still able to choke out, "We were buddies. He spoke about Nicole a lot, so I decided to look her up."

"Ah, I see." The expression in Colleen's eyes shifted to one of understanding. "That's very sweet of you."

She wouldn't think so once he told her his true reasons for being here. "There's more." He paused, wondering how to proceed. Unable to think of an easy segue, he just ventured forth. "In fact, I was with him when he died." *Too much information*, his inner voice screamed. "He asked me to make sure Nicole was okay."

Colleen's gaze reverted to the previous one of suspicion. "But why now? It's been almost a year since Seth died."

Cam shrugged. "Better late than never. Don't you think?" He glanced at the carpet, not particularly pleased to come across as a smartass, but he couldn't look her in the eye and admit to being a coward.

"Hmm. Maybe." Colleen tapped her foot. When she crossed her arms, the movement drew his attention. His focus slowly moved higher. Again, her gaze seemed to be taking in his every detail, as if he were a legal document written in fine print.

After more seconds of silent scrutiny, she said, "So, Cam. Tell me a little about yourself."

"Excuse me?" Somehow she'd turned the tables on him.

"Call me overprotective if you must, but I need to look out for my daughter's best interests. So before I introduce you, I'd like to get to know you." She slipped out from behind the counter. "In fact, let's have a cup of hot cocoa and if you like sweets, I'm sure you'll love the éclairs we serve to our customers."

"But I'm not a customer," he stammered, feeling a little stuck. This *so* wasn't going his way.

"You will be."

Uh-oh. Cam swallowed hard. The confidence in the statement concerned him. The smile that suddenly took over her face was just a little too mischievous for his comfort. It was like his mother's smile when she was fixated on something.

"Nicole's at lunch and won't be back for another forty-five minutes. That gives us plenty of time to chat."

Damn. He should have known she'd be at lunch. Cam squirmed, ignoring the desire to turn around and never look back. Instead, he followed Colleen to a couple of tables and chairs off to the side of the showroom. After all, she seemed like a nice lady, and he needed to do whatever was necessary to get the job done.

A customer entered the shop.

Colleen called to the back room, "Maggie, Mrs. Emerson is here. Can you come out and help her? I'm busy."

"Sure thing." Another lady, presumably Maggie, bustled out. "Good afternoon, Mrs. Emerson," she said with much enthusiasm. "Merry Christmas. How have you been?"

While Maggie and Mrs. Emerson talked, Cam sat in one of the chairs that Colleen had pulled out.

"What have you been doing since you got back from Afghanistan?" She poured hot chocolate from a large thermos into one of two cups.

It seemed like an easy enough question to answer without giving too much away, so Cam explained about his injury as she put a pastry on a plate. He then went on to tell her how after he'd been discharged, he'd used his medical training to become an EMT.

She set both the hot chocolate and éclair in front of him and then made herself comfortable in a seat across from him.

While they ate, he talked more about his current job and his future goals. That was something he could easily share. In fact, it was better if she knew how busy he was. That way, she might cut him some slack with her daughter. "As an EMT, I work three twelve-hour shifts a week, and my schedule allows me to finish school."

"I'm so glad you're continuing your education." Her smile radiated warmth. For some reason, Cam rather liked having this woman's approval. "My husband and I encouraged all of our children to get one. Knowledge is power and paves the way to a better life."

Colleen spent a few minutes telling him about her "brood," as she called it. Her life with nine kids sounded like one of those old sitcoms where everything was perfect. An only child, he'd love to have a bunch of brothers and sisters. His only extended family of an uncle, two aunts, and many cousins lived in Mexico. From their limited conversation, it was obvious the Murphys weren't rich like Seth's family, but they weren't poor like Cam's family either.

"This, along with the conversation, was worth the trip over," he said, holding up the last of the éclair. He took the bite of pastry, washing it down with the rest of the cocoa. "Thanks."

Another lady entered the shop. Maggie was at the register, still working with Mrs. Emerson.

"I'll be right with you," Maggie said as Colleen picked up the empty dishes and placed them on a tray in the back corner.

Cam rose. Not wanting to get in the way when there was a paying customer present, he said, "Go ahead. I'll just look around while I wait."

"You're a sweet boy." Colleen gave him another approving smile that would make anyone feel ten feet tall before she hurried away. Unfortunately, she had no idea of his true nature. He was neither sweet nor a boy.

Colleen Murphy was a really nice lady. If the daughter was anything like the mother, Cam could see why Seth sang her praises so often.

Like most guys, jewelry didn't thrill him. Still, he now took more notice of the displays filled with necklaces, bracelets, and earrings. It was hard not to, considering their appeal. One in particular caught his eye.

He stepped closer to the showcase to get a better look at some shiny earrings his mother would like.

"Are you considering buying something?" Colleen said, coming up behind him. Her customer was just leaving. "For your girlfriend, maybe?"

"No." Despite the curiosity in her voice or the interest shining in her eyes, Cam didn't enlighten her as to his single status. Once she got to know him better, she'd lose all interest—especially if she was thinking of hooking him up with one of her daughters. The ladies at his mother's assisted-living complex were always trying to do that. "My mother would love these for their simplicity."

"Oh?"

Cam shook his head. "But Mom wouldn't want me spending money on something so frivolous." Once he completed his studies, he planned to take her to Mexico to see her brother and two sisters. What little he had left over after paying bills had been set aside for that trip.

"Everyone likes frivolous things now and then. Even mothers." Colleen took the earrings out and set them on a velvet pad.

Though a simple teardrop design, they really were quite beautiful. Torn, he picked one up and studied it. Unfortunately, his mother's voice was inside his head, saying she had nowhere to wear such pretty things. He said, "Mom lives at Windsor Manor and they provide all of her needs, so she rarely goes out now." Back when his mom still worked, they would go out regularly and have fun. Now he didn't have the funds or the time for anything other than his biweekly visits.

"Your mother sounds lovely. And someone like that deserves to have something pretty." She paused. "I'll tell you what, I'll give these to you at cost."

Colleen named a figure that Cam would be a fool to turn down. Still, it didn't seem right that she'd be out a profit.

As he opened his mouth to say so, she cut him off. "Really, it's okay." The sincerity in her voice added to her urging.

Nodding, he held out his hand. "You have a deal."

Of course his mom would balk at his Christmas gift, but so what? She *did* deserve the earrings. Conchetta Camareno had worked her tail off cleaning rich women's houses her entire life. If nothing else, she could just wear them to the formal dining room at Windsor Manor when he was her guest. Cam ate there at least once a week. After all, his agreement with the facility included the extra meals at no charge.

The two walked to the register where Colleen rang up the sale. "I like you, Cam," she said, handing him the earrings now boxed and bagged. "And because I do, I'm going to do you a favor."

"A favor, huh?" What was it about moms and favors,

anyway? Cam eyed her intently, wondering the whole time if it had been a mistake to come here after all.

"Okay, maybe the favor is more for me," she admitted.

Having already figured that out, he sighed. Now he was sure the lady was up to something. Lord, he hoped she wasn't planning on fixing him up with one of her daughters.

"Nicole needs a date for an event this Saturday night."

He stared at her openmouthed, totally not expecting the daughter to be Nicole.

She put up a hand. "Hear me out before you say no."

At this point, he was too dumbstruck to do anything else but listen.

The door flew open and Nicole burst inside. "I'm back."

Both turned her way and she stopped short. "Oh, I didn't know you had a customer."

Maggie had gone into the back room as soon as Mrs. Emerson had departed.

"No problem, sweetie. I was just telling this young man about your cause, and he's agreed to help." Colleen patted his shoulder.

"My cause?" she said at the same time he blurted, "Her cause?" *Damn.* Suddenly he felt as if there were a noose around his neck.

"Yes," Colleen said to Nicole. "You need a date. And"—her nod indicated him—"he needs somewhere to take his mother."

"Wait, wait." Cam shook his head to clear it and held up a hand. Was this lady nuts? He glanced at Nicole and their gazes locked. In that brief moment a connection was made, one that zinged all the way to his gut. At least, that was what it felt like to him—an instant attraction for want of a better term—which seemed stupid considering he wasn't one to fall under anyone's spell, especially so quickly. And this woman was definitely off-limits.

Cam took a deep breath to clear his mind. Seth's Nicole had beautiful eyes. Eyes that drew him in and made him want the unattainable.

Uncomfortable with his reaction, he turned to Colleen. "My

mom won't go." This was obviously the favor she'd mentioned, but one look at Nicole and he knew it wasn't a good idea.

"Why not?" Hands on her hips, Colleen gave him a stern look that said she expected him to at the very least talk his mom into it. "It's for a good cause, and the tickets have already been purchased."

"Will you stop, Mom?" Frowning, Nicole went to put her jacket away.

Colleen leaned in and whispered, "Please? Don't make me beg."

"I—" Cam ran a hand through his hair and rested it on the back of his neck. Her words were hard enough to brush aside, but ignoring that pleading stare was more than a challenge. Hell, he didn't even own a car. How was he supposed to take both his mother and Nicole to some event without one?

"And don't tell her you're here because Seth asked you to come. That will only upset her. This means a great deal to me," she said.

Nodding, he felt more than a twinge of dread as his gaze drifted to the woman breezing back into the showroom like a breath of fresh air, before it landed on her mother again. The entire time his mind waged a bitter battle. Seth had wanted him to take care of Nicole, and Cam wanted nothing more than to do that for his fallen friend. But he'd just been tossed into deep water without a life vest. Now if he honored his promise, things could get dicey.

Nicole Murphy was one in a million. To say he hadn't been struck with a lightning bolt of attraction was a bald-faced lie. And if his radar was correct, she'd felt something for him. The eyes never lied about shit like that. That thought alone was enough to cause him to break out in a cold sweat.

Attraction for a guy like him, one who had nothing to offer, was a dead-end street for both of them.

Chapter 5

Mom had gone too far this time. Nicole rushed over to Colleen and the man who was obviously being coerced into a blind date with her.

"Don't worry," Nicole said, meeting his gaze. "I'll take care of this." She turned to her mother, ignoring the spark of . . . attraction? Interest? Whatever it was, she didn't like it.

"Mom, can I speak with you?" She grabbed her mother's arm. "Privately," she said pointedly, pulling Colleen with her while heading toward the back room. Over her shoulder, she added, "We won't be long."

When they were out of earshot, Nicole practically hissed, "What is *wrong* with you?"

"What do you mean, dear?" Her mom could give lessons on how to look innocent.

"Don't play dumb with me," she said, resisting the urge to stomp her foot. "You know exactly what I mean." With her hands on her hips, she narrowed her gaze. "You're trying to set me up with that man, and I won't stand for it."

"No, honey, you're wrong. He came into the store and bought a gift for his mother. We got to talking, and I realized he's one of those wounded vets your organization tries to help." Colleen shrugged. "What better way to help him than to get him to attend the gala?"

Nicole groaned, reaching for patience. Just how gullible did her mother think she was? "He's not disabled."

"Some disabilities are buried deep in the mind and aren't visible." Colleen patted her shoulder. "Besides, he's taking his mother, not you. Mrs. Camareno lives in an assisted-living facility and doesn't get out much." Her expression turned pleading. "I merely thought you could befriend him. You know . . . take him under your wing, so to speak, and help him." This time her look was more convincing and harder to ignore.

Nicole eyed her mom speculatively, and then quickly glanced at the man patiently waiting by the display of bracelets. He *was* handsome . . . She jerked her thoughts back on track. It made sense in a peculiar Colleen Murphy kind of way. "But what if he doesn't really want to go?"

"Well, that's why I included you. I'm sure he'd agree to go with you if he thought you needed a date." Her eyes filled with concern. "But I understand if you'd rather not." Colleen gazed at a spot beyond Nicole's shoulder. "Maybe I can ask Suzie Rockwell," she murmured, mentioning a neighbor, someone Nicole didn't particularly care for.

"Oh, that'll really be good for his mental health." Suzie was a *love 'em and leave 'em* kind of woman. "She'll just rein him in and once she's had her fill, spit the leftovers out as if he didn't have feelings."

"I doubt that will happen. He's too busy to form any kind of attachment to her, or any woman for that matter."

"How can you be so sure?" Suddenly interested, Nicole needed to know.

"He said as much. Working thirty-six hours a week and managing a full load at college eats into his social life. Homework, overtime, and his visits to his mother take up practically the whole twenty-four hours of his day. A night out might do him good."

"I see." Nicole nodded. If he was as busy as her mom said, maybe it wouldn't be so bad to have him and his mother tag along with her. After all, there was something appealing . . .

No! She wasn't going there. To even consider it felt like a betrayal to Seth.

"Seth's gone," her mother said, as if she'd just read her thoughts. "It's okay to go out and have some fun with a good-looking man like Cam."

"Cam? That's his name?" She rather liked it.

"It's really Roberto, but he goes by Cam."

Nicole grinned. "Maybe you should go with him then. Since you're on good enough terms to call him by a nickname."

"Oh, for heaven's sake." Colleen threw up her hands. "He's a lonely vet who could use an evening out. Just like you. What harm can come of it?"

When she put it like that, it did make her seem pretty callous to ignore his plight. "Okay." Nicole nodded. "But I'm only going along with it because his mother is coming as well." At least that idea provided a modicum of protection. As soon as the thought was out, she discarded it. What did she need protecting from? Certainly not from a guy like Cam—one her mother picked out, at that.

"Thanks." Colleen wrapped her in a bear hug. "I really appreciate this, and I know he will too, once he sees how happy his mother is when she gets out for a night on the town."

Her mother let go and Nicole felt a confusing sense of loss. Since Seth's death, she rarely hugged anyone. Now it seemed she craved human contact. Maybe she was finally coming to grips with his death.

Remembering the look in Cam's eyes when their gazes had locked, a tiny thrill went through her. At this point, she decided not to lie and pretend the man wasn't attractive. It didn't mean anything. Heck, lots of men had looked at her like that in the last year. *Yeah*, her conscience answered. *But none of those guys had you responding to the look.*

Ridiculous, she shot back mentally. That only meant she was ready to move on with her life. A sense of joy filled her at the thought. Her grin widened. Who knew that the mere thought of a date with a hunk—despite the fact that it included the guy's mom—would achieve such a feat? *Ah! So he's a hunk*, her mind shouted.

Nicole quieted the voices in her head and looked at her mother. "Let's see if we can twist his arm into going on Saturday night."

Colleen's smile matched hers. "You won't regret it."

Lord, she hoped not. The approval in Colleen's expression should have warned her. But already guilt over finding another man attractive chipped away at her newfound resolve. Maybe she wasn't ready, after all. As her mom grabbed her hand and headed toward the showroom, the reality of the situation kicked in. Oh God, what had she done?

Unfortunately, the die was cast and there was no backing out now. Nicole swallowed hard and sent up a silent message. *Sorry, Seth. It's for a good cause.*

• • •

Cam paced back and forth, every once in a while checking the spot where Colleen and her daughter had left only moments ago. Hopefully, Nicole had straightened things out. He sure wished she would hurry, though. He didn't know how long he could hold out now that Maggie, the other salesperson, had jumped into the game.

"Nicole has worked hard for the gala," Maggie said. She'd come up to him as the other two had left and had begun singing Nicole's praises. "She's sequestered herself since Seth's death, and it's not good for her. Maybe if she thought she was helping you by going with you?"

She thinks I need help? Sheesh. Cam barely refrained from rolling his eyes and nodded politely. "My mom—"

"Will love it," Maggie said, cutting him off. "You know she would."

She had him there. Hell, she'd outmaneuvered him more quickly than a general with a full army. He scrubbed his face with his hands, wishing he'd never listened to his conscience last night.

What if Seth's Nicole agreed to this craziness? He didn't think he had the will to deny her, especially if she locked gazes with him again. *Shit.* Just thinking about it had his heart pumping in double-time. *Stay strong*, he thought. *And don't look into her eyes.* If he could do that, he could avoid a catastrophe.

Colleen and her daughter made an appearance through the door they'd exited earlier.

Without listening to his mind's reasoning, his gaze sought Nicole's. And again, when their eyes fastened on each other's, it was like a sucker punch to the gut. He was in deep, because no amount of reasoning was going to stop him from agreeing to Colleen's request. It was only one night, after all. Once it was over, Nicole would go her way and he'd go his.

And wasn't that a big fat lie.

He'd promised Seth he'd look after her. A quick glance at the ceiling, and he sent up a silent prayer. *Okay, Seth, this is what you asked for on the day you died—and on every occasion that you've haunted me. I'm only doing my duty to you and to her.*

The attraction didn't mean a thing. He couldn't help his reaction after connecting stares with a beautiful woman. Hell, he was only flesh and blood.

As he left the shop, Cam walked taller, confident that he could handle a little attraction. Things would work out as they should.

• • •

Cam rapped on the door and let himself into the apartment. "Hi, Mom."

Conchetta Camareno smiled from where she stood at the kitchen sink, dressed in what she termed her native costume.

"*Hola*, Roberto." Reverting to Spanish as she sometimes did, she asked how he was.

"*Bien*." He paused briefly to take in her outfit and nodded. "You look pretty."

His mother looked down at her clothing, practically blushing. "I like wearing colorful skirts and blouses. I've decided to do it more often."

Her collarless blouse rimmed her petite shoulders. Together with her flowing cotton skirt that hit mid-calf, she appeared delicate and feminine. Definitely not sixty years old, and much too young to allow life to pass her by. Conchetta's arthritis made it difficult to do a lot of things, but there were just as many that she could still manage, especially if she took her pain medication and did her stretches.

Cam finally understood what Colleen had meant. "I have a favor to ask."

"Oh?" She turned off the tap, leaving the jug used to water

her beloved plants in the sink for him to manage, and gave him her full attention.

Drawing near, he kissed her cheek, then picked up the jug. "I've been invited to a night out, and I want you to go with me."

Based on the quick interest in her eyes, he could tell the idea appealed to her. But rather than agree, she shook her head. "I don't think so, *mi niño.*"

"You haven't even heard what it is and you're already declining?" he said while watering the plants near the window. Once done, he set the jug under the sink for his next visit.

He went up to his mom and placed his hands on her shoulders to gain her full attention. "What if I told you it's important to me?" He then explained about the gala. After a bit of online research, he'd found a company that rented cars by the hour without breaking his budget.

Conchetta again shook her head and offered an emphatic no. "I'd feel uncomfortable," she said. "First of all, I have nothing to wear, and secondly, I won't know anyone."

He wasn't sure he was relieved or disappointed, but at least he'd tried. Seth had to be content with that. Glancing toward the heavens, he prayed it was so.

On his way home, he texted Colleen to tell her. As he typed in the last word, a sense of loss filled him. Since he'd left Mary Ann's shop, his anticipation for the upcoming weekend had grown. It didn't escape his notice that he hadn't felt this way about anything in a long, long time.

Chapter 6

"Can you believe he's turned us down?" Colleen said to Maggie after reading the text. Her shoulders slumped and disappointment deflated some of her holiday spirit. "I thought he was the answer to our prayers."

"What reason did he give?"

"His mother would feel uncomfortable. Plus she has nothing suitable to wear."

Maggie looked at her sharply. "And you're settling for that pitiful excuse?"

"Of course it's an excuse." Having worked the kinks out of her shoulder, she went back to adding more decorative ribbon to one of the cases, redoing what Mary Ann had stripped out earlier. "And no, I'm not settling for anything less than seeing them at the gala. I propose a mission of mercy."

Maggie rubbed her hands together, clearly enjoying the idea of a mission. "What did you have in mind?"

"We need to go and see her."

As soon as Mary Ann relieved them, they hopped into Colleen's old Mercury and drove to San Jose, following the Google Map instructions she'd typed into her cell phone.

Colleen pulled into the parking lot. "It looks like a nice place." She turned off the ignition and glanced at Maggie.

"What? Why are you looking at me like that? I'm never going to live in one of those places."

Colleen grunted, a not-so-ladylike sound. "Have you ever been in one?"

"No, can't say as I have." She hopped out. As Colleen followed, Maggie waited until the two met on the sidewalk. Her gaze swept the buildings in front of her. "But it does look like an apartment complex.''

It did. The center building was three stories, constructed of pink brick with white trim. Condos and townhouses surrounded it, just like any complex that rented apartments. "Only difference is this is for the senior crowd, not the single crowd."

Maggie started walking. "Well, I'm both, and I still wouldn't be caught dead here."

"Shush," Colleen warned as the double doors opened when they stepped close enough. "Someone will hear you."

As they entered what was obviously the main entrance, Maggie slowed, studying every aspect of the huge reception room on the right that looked like it belonged in a mansion in Palm Beach. Colleen's heels tapped a staccato beat on the tile floor. The sound echoed as she walked up to the wraparound unit on their left, one that appeared similar to a hospital or doctor's office sign-in station.

The lady behind the desk looked up. "May I help you?"

"Yes." Colleen offered her warmest smile. "We're here to see Mrs. Camareno. Can you tell us where we need to go?"

The woman, resembling Nurse Ratched with a bad attitude, didn't return the smile. "Mrs. Camareno is in unit 3825." She pointed to the elevator. "Third floor. Turn right when you get off." Then she shoved a book in front of her. "First, you have to sign in."

"She's a prisoner, for God's sake," Maggie whispered into her ear, having come to stand beside her.

"I beg your pardon?" Judging by her tone, Nurse Ratched couldn't be more offended. "Windsor Manor is not a prison. We take great pride in the care we provide our clientele." She looked down her nose at Colleen, then Maggie, her expression saying they would never meet the criteria for being considered as clientele. "Our facilities are top notch, and the care impeccable."

"Of course they are. We didn't mean to imply otherwise." Colleen had a hard time keeping her smile intact. She signed both their names and grabbed Maggie's arm. "Thanks for your help. I'm sure we'll find Mrs. Camareno's apartment."

She hit the elevator call button and turned back around.

Nurse Ratched was watching them as if they were teens bent on shoplifting. Nodding, she jabbed the button several times in an effort to bring the car faster.

"Am I right, or am I wrong?" Maggie asked, once the doors closed off the woman's disapproving gaze. "Prison with a capital P."

Though it did feel a little bit confining, Colleen shook her head. "We shouldn't judge without knowing all the facts."

Maggie crossed her arms and harrumphed. "The idea of someone having to sign in to see me if I were in one of these places is reason enough to stay out of them."

"You might change your mind once you get older."

"I doubt it."

"Your fear of aging is showing again."

Maggie stared straight ahead, acting as if she hadn't heard.

Typical, Colleen thought as the doors opened. Her friend was into anything and everything if it helped her stay youthful, as long as it didn't require surgery.

They exited the elevator and turned right. Following the apartment numbers, they finally came to 3825. "This place even smells like a prison."

"You're just being contrary. You have no idea what a prison smells like, and you know it." Colleen threw her a withering look. "Now hush or you can wait in the car."

"I'll be good. You need me along for moral support."

"Then keep your mouth shut and let me do the talking." Colleen rapped on the door.

The door opened a crack, and a petite Hispanic woman peeked through the small gap. "Yes?"

"Mrs. Camareno?" When she nodded, Colleen added, "We're friends of your son, Roberto. I'm Colleen, and this is Maggie," she said, gesturing to her friend at her side.

The lady sized them up a moment before standing to the side and opening the door wider. "And I'm Conchetta. Won't you please come in?"

Colleen followed Maggie inside the cozy apartment that was as nice as Nicole's studio apartment, yet much roomier. The coral and aqua accents used throughout lightened the dark wood flooring and lent a Southwestern flair to the decor. Colleen liked what she saw because it defined Cam's mom as someone who wanted to show off her heritage.

Conchetta led them to a leather sofa, the color reminding Colleen of the red rocks of Sedona, Arizona. "Please sit down and make yourselves comfortable," she said in a thick Hispanic accent. Her eyebrows arched. "Would you like something to drink?"

"No, thanks." Colleen sat and tried to think of a way to begin the conversation.

"We're here on a mission," Maggie said, obviously not paying any attention to her demand that she remain silent. A good thing too, because Maggie had Conchetta's complete attention.

"We're the meddling old ladies who invited Cam to this gala event on Saturday." Maggie went on to explain what it was for and how they had extra tickets. She ended with, "We think it's important for both Cam and Nicole to go together."

The older woman's brows knit together. "I don't understand. When I ask him, he says he's not interested in dating right now." Her confused gaze remained on Maggie a while before traveling to Colleen, then finally back to Maggie. "Why would attending this fiesta change his mind?"

"You weren't there to catch the signals pinging back and forth between the two young people, but we were. And I must say they were—"

"I'll be blunt," Colleen chimed in, quickly cutting off her friend. "Nicole was engaged to Cam's best friend. Since Seth died, she's been desolate, and now a year later, she's not getting any better." She hesitated long enough to gauge the woman's reaction. When her expression said go on, Colleen cleared her throat and added, "I can't be sure, but Cam seems like he could use a fun evening out too."

"Yes, I understand what you are implying. My Cam isn't the same since returning from his last duty. I miss his smile, his laughter. He takes good care of me, but hides his pain. And now since I have fallen a few times, he is burdened even more. I thank

God I have this home. It puts his mind at ease. No one should be a burden to their children."

"Isn't that our payback for what we mothers went through during labor?"

"Stop it, Maggie. She doesn't know you're just joking."

"I'm sorry." The gleam in Maggie's eyes brightened as she leaned forward, gently grasping Conchetta's hands. "Anyone who knows me knows I dote on my son, his wife, and my grandbaby. I guess I can't say things like that until we become better acquainted."

"Getting back on track." Colleen flashed Maggie a look that said *stay quiet*. "You have to attend, and we're not leaving here until you agree."

"I have nothing to wear." The small woman glanced down, pressing her skirt with her hands.

"Ah, ah, ah." Colleen wagged a finger. "That's the same excuse Nicole tried to use. We'll find you something to wear."

Conchetta thought about this for a moment before exhaling a long sigh. "You really think this will help my *niño*?"

"If you mean Cam, then yes. It will help."

"Then I have no choice." She stood, but it obviously took a little effort, even with the help of a cane. "But I don't want to embarrass my boy. I really don't have anything to wear to such a glamorous party."

Wearing a triumphant grin, Maggie jumped up. "We know all the right places to shop."

"I can't afford much. I live on a fixed budget."

"Girl, have you ever heard of nearly-new shops?" Standing, Colleen waved a hand in the air. "Those snooty women in the hills of Saratoga and Santa Clara County hate to wear anything twice."

"Careful," Maggie warned. "You're talking about my son and daughter-in-law."

"No, I'm not. Judith is too practical to sell an outfit, even after only wearing it half a dozen times." After tossing her friend another *butt-out* glare, Colleen returned to Cam's mom. "Anyway, as I was saying, some of these women sell their clothes at secondhand stores for next to nothing. I Googled a few before I came."

"She's gone Google crazy since I showed her how to use it," Maggie explained when Conchetta's expression turned questioning. "In fact, I may have created a Google-using monster."

"Oh, hush. Don't listen to her." Colleen started for the door. "Once we find you a dress to wear at a price you can afford, then we'll have to work on Cam."

"Don't worry about him. I'll make sure he goes." Conchetta's conspiratorial tone suggested they had her full cooperation. "As long as it will help him get back to his old self—and his smile returns—I'll do what I can."

"Great." Colleen held the door open. "Then what are we waiting for?"

The three headed out. At the desk, Nurse Ratched gave Conchetta the same disapproving look. "Don't forget to sign out and put how long you'll be."

"Definitely a prison," Maggie whispered to Colleen so no one else could hear. Once outside, Maggie glanced at Conchetta. "What happens if you're late?"

"I don't know. I rarely go out."

"Oh, you poor thing." Maggie wrapped an arm around the older woman's shoulders and peered up at Colleen. "We'll just have to remedy that, won't we?"

Colleen grinned. "We can add her to our bingo night."

Allowing Maggie to lead her to the car, Conchetta gave a slight shake of the head. "I have no transportation."

"No problem." Maggie halted at Colleen's car. "You're not too far from my house. I can swing by and pick you up, then drop you back home afterward. I guarantee you'll love it."

As Colleen pointed her key fob and clicked, Conchetta said, "We have bingo nights here."

"You'll have much more fun with us." Maggie opened the door and helped the older lady get seated inside the vehicle.

"It seems like too much trouble for you to go to." Brow furrowed, Conchetta shook her head.

"You might as well give in," Colleen said, cutting off what Maggie was about to say next. "Once she gets fixated on an idea, she treats it like a dog with a bone that hasn't eaten in a month. She'll just whittle away your objections until they're gone."

Conchetta glanced at Maggie, her gaze assessing. Finally, she nodded. "Okay. I'd like that. I think."

Maggie's smile was almost gloating as she helped her fasten her seat belt. "You won't be sorry." She climbed into the backseat.

"Thank God you agreed in record time." Colleen gave Cam's mother a conspiratorial wink and started the car. "Otherwise, Maggie gets a little annoying."

Rolling her eyes, Maggie grunted. "Let's focus on finding our new friend a dress, rather than disparaging my character." She snapped her seat belt into place. "Then we can move on to stage two of our plans."

"Stage two?" Conchetta slanted a glance at Colleen, then at Maggie in the rearview mirror.

"Convincing Cam that you want to go," Maggie replied.

As if she finally decided to play along, a grinning Conchetta nodded. "You can very well leave that up to me."

Chapter 7

Cam rapped on Nicole's apartment door.

He pulled at the collar of his starched white shirt. If only it didn't fit quite so snugly. It chafed, and the tie was like a noose around his neck. He couldn't remember the last time he'd dared to dress up in a monkey suit. On the other hand, he did like looking his best in something other than a uniform. If he were honest with himself, he'd even admit his aim was to impress a certain lady, which made absolutely no sense, even if it was appropriate.

The door opened. The pleased expression on Nicole's face would be etched into his memory forever. The admiration in her eyes made him throw back his shoulders and stand taller.

"My, you do clean up nicely, Mr. Camareno." She glanced around. "Your mother?"

"In the car. And call me Cam." The light banter put him at ease. "And so do you, I might add."

Her brows drew together.

"Look very nice." He did a little twirling thing with his hand. "Turn around so I can see the whole effect."

Obliging him, she pivoted slowly. The iridescent green material followed, outlining her lush figure. "Do I pass?"

"Let's just say if your score was any higher, I'd run out of numbers." He grinned. "In other words, you look beautiful."

"Thank you."

Her warm smile added to her beauty. So much so that she took his breath away. But that didn't ease his mind. No, he was here to look after her—not *at* her—just as he'd promised.

She handed him her shawl that obviously went with her evening gown. Taking his time, he placed the garment around her shoulders. Once done, he clenched his hands into fists to still the urge to pull her closer.

Wouldn't do to scare her away before he'd even had the chance to fulfill his task. *Remember, you're not here to flirt.* Over and over he repeated the statement, using it as a mental mantra in order to keep on track as they walked side by side down the silent hallway. With every step, the swishing sound from her dress, along with the fact that their shoulders touched every now and then, had him a little off-kilter. As the elevator doors closed, he exhaled a long breath. If he didn't get his emotions under control, it was going to be a long, long night.

Thankfully, the trip to the first floor took only seconds. In no time they were outside, heading in the direction of his car where he could breathe easier.

When his mom saw their approach, she started to climb out of the Nissan Altima that one of the guys at the fire station had offered after hearing where Cam had planned on taking his mother. Not having to rent a car worked for him, saving him both time and money.

"You should have waited for me to help you," Cam said, hurrying up to his mom to give her a steady hand. "What's more, you didn't need to get out."

"I wanted to meet your date properly." She turned to Nicole and smiled.

Cam sighed. Sometimes it was next to impossible to keep her from doing and saying exactly what was on her mind. He indicated Nicole with the tilt of his head. "Mom, I'd like you to meet Nicole Murphy."

"It's a pleasure," she said, reaching for Nicole's outstretched hand.

"Same here, Mrs. Camareno."

"Please, call me Conchetta."

Nicole nodded. "I love what you're wearing. It's unique and lovely."

Conchetta practically blushed as she did a slow spin, showing off her attire. With her teal full skirt and ivory blouse that left her shoulders and neck bare, she looked like a Spanish princess. His mother had never appeared so animated. A twinge of guilt rode up his spine. Why hadn't he figured out on his own that she might enjoy getting out more?

When Cam helped Conchetta climb into the backseat, Nicole placed a hand on her shoulder. "Why don't you take the front seat?"

"Not to worry. I rather like pretending I'm being chauffeured around." She laughed. "Makes me feel important, like one of the ladies I used to clean for."

With his mom seated, Cam waited until Nicole was inside before closing both doors and running around to the driver's side. The community center where the gala was taking place was less than ten minutes away. Once there, he ushered the women in, one on each arm, as the valet parked the car.

"Oh my. Isn't it festive?" Conchetta's voice held a touch of awe as she gazed around.

Cam nodded. It looked like a winter wonderland. There were Christmas decorations on every table. Green garlands with silver and gold ornaments were draped along the walls. In the center toward the front was a large dance floor. A live band played in an alcove behind the dancers.

An older lady spotted them from across the room and made a beeline in their direction.

"I'm glad you came," she said to Nicole. Then she turned to Cam and his mother. "I don't think we've met." She held out a hand. "I'm Mrs. Jones, chairperson for A Healing Christmas."

Nicole cleared her throat. She glanced at Cam. "This is Roberto Camareno and his mother, Conchetta Camareno," she said, indicating Cam's mom with a gesture.

Mrs. Jones placed a hand on the older lady's arm. "Mrs. Camareno, I have someone I'd like you to meet. That way we can let these two youngsters enjoy themselves without feeling like they have to entertain us."

"Call me Conchetta," she said, laughing.

They walked off with Mrs. Jones's arm still around Conchetta as her voice carried. "And you must call me Mildred."

Pursing her lips, Nicole slanted a glance toward him. "Well, I guess you're stuck with me."

"Is that a problem?" His gaze narrowed as he studied her features.

"No," she replied much too quickly for him to believe her. Plus there was the fact that as the band played on, Nicole fidgeted. Her hands were constantly in motion as were her feet, as she stepped from one to the other.

Did he make her as nervous as she made him? The thought brought a slight tug to his lips.

"What's so funny?"

Startled to hear her voice, he met her gaze. She must have been watching him to notice his slight smile. His lips curled into a wider grin. "I was just thinking that this crowd makes me nervous," he admitted.

Part of it was true. Nicole didn't need to know that ninety-nine percent of his nervousness was due to one particular lady in the crowd, standing so close he could smell her perfume. He didn't recognize the scent, not that he was a connoisseur of perfumes. Still, the flowery tanginess suited her. He stifled the urge to lean closer and inhale deeper. That wouldn't be cool. He hadn't dated in the last year. Hell, for that matter he could count on one hand the number of women he'd taken out in the last five years, so his dating etiquette was a little stale.

Somehow he had to put her at ease. And the only way to do that was to relax himself by breaking the ice.

The music changed to a familiar beat. "Shall we?" He held out his hand to indicate the dance floor.

Nicole's eyebrows inched closer together. "This is a salsa."

"So?"

"So, I've never done one."

"Really?" That surprised him, considering it seemed to be the craze for a while.

Drawing back, she said, "Does that change your opinion of me?"

He laughed. "I prefer to postpone any opinion forming until after the dance."

She rolled her eyes. "Oh, great. That really makes me feel

more confident."

"It's not hard, especially if you have a partner who knows how to lead."

"And I suppose you do?"

"Well . . ." Cam bowed. "Without being immodest, I'd have to answer in the affirmative. I lead a pretty mean salsa." Thanks to his mother, who loved to dance.

He spent a few minutes showing her the basic steps. "The turns and other steps are little more intricate, but if you keep to the rhythm, I won't be hard to follow." Placing one hand on her waist, he gripped hers with the other. "Here, let me show you. One, two, three, four." Over and over, he demonstrated the main steps, and she easily kept up.

"Now for the hard part," he murmured, leading her into an easy turn. "Just relax and follow my cues."

The lively music continued and so did he. "There you have it."

She was a natural.

Laughing, Nicole tossed her head back. "By George, I think I do." She showed off and twisted her body to the steps, the entire time rolling her hips from side to side.

Cam had a hard time concentrating on his own steps, too distracted by what those hips were doing. She had a lithe body and an easy rhythm. As the music died, disappointment filled him.

He could dance with her all night.

Cheeks red from exertion, she waved a hand in front of her face. "Whoa, that was fun, but I'm parched."

"What would you like to drink?" As Nicole replied, he searched the crowd for his mother, and spied her in a group of older people. She was laughing at something the man next to her had just said. Her earrings danced when she moved her head. His mom wore his Christmas present, something that he'd insisted she open ahead of time so she could wear them with her pretty outfit.

From this distance, it looked as if they were flirting with each other. Cam grinned as he headed for the bar. His mother looked happy. She deserved to have distinguished gentlemen paying attention to her.

"What'll it be?" the bartender said, wiping the bar with a damp cloth.

"A chardonnay, please."

"You're not having anything?" Nicole had obviously followed.

Cam glanced at the man. "And a water." Then turning back to her, he said, "I rarely drink anything stronger than a beer now and then."

"Really?"

Her question seemed to require an explanation. Shrugging, he said, "My dad was an alcoholic who was drunk when he died." Why hide the fact? He ignored the notion that his blunt honesty might very well be a means to scare her away and added, "One of the worst experiences of my life involved drinking too much as a teen, and because alcoholism runs in families, I decided why risk it?"

"I didn't mean to pry."

But rather than fear or disdain, her expression held only curiosity, which meant his ploy backfired. He paid for her drink, handed her the wine, and picked up his water that the bartender had placed in front of him. "We're in luck. There's an empty table."

He pulled out a chair for Nicole, then sat beside her.

"So, how did you learn to salsa like that?" she asked with a bit of awe in her voice as if the last thirty seconds hadn't happened.

In response, Cam sat taller and grinned. "My mom. She always said women liked to dance, and if I wanted pretty girls to like me, I should learn."

"You're lucky. Neither of my parents is into dancing." Nicole concentrated on her wineglass. Her fingers sliding up and down the stem drew his gaze. "Did you take lessons?" she asked without looking up.

"No." Cam's reply must have held some hint of his newfound reluctance to talk about his past, which only seemed to increase her interest. The glance she slanted at him said, *There's more to the story, so spill.* Unable to resist the look, he shrugged. "After my dad died, money was scarce."

Growing up poor wasn't a crime. Besides, maybe he just hadn't shared enough about his youth. Giving her the whole picture might do the trick and act as a barrier between them. The air practically snapped with tension born of awareness of each other. His attraction to her was hard enough to ignore without adding hers into the mix.

"Mom spent a lot of Saturday nights showing me the steps." He smiled at the memory of the two of them in their tiny kitchen. He then went on to explain how Conchetta had worked as a cleaning lady. They barely had enough to get by until Cam turned sixteen and got a job.

Nicole was easy to talk to. In fact, Cam had never revealed so much about those early years to any other woman. Her probing questions, asked in such an innocuous way, had sliced away his natural reserve.

In turn, she spent a great deal of time talking about her upbringing. He already had an idea of what her life had been like, thanks to Colleen, but hearing it from her lips made it seem more idyllic.

"I'd love to have so many brothers and sisters."

"Not if you had to be somewhere in the morning and both bathrooms were full."

"I gather that took planning."

"I just used to get up early and shower. That way I had plenty of time to put on my makeup and do my hair without being disturbed."

"I doubt that took long with your beauty."

Jeez, Cam, he thought. *Just come out with the lame comments, why don't you?* When she blushed and peered at him through half-lidded eyes, he swallowed hard.

"You think so?"

The uncertainty in her voice tugged on his heartstrings. She had to know how attractive she was.

"Yes, I do," he said, just in case she didn't.

Another jolt of awareness passed between them. Cam wanted to sit there all night and bask in her gaze, but someone shoved into his shoulders.

"Excuse me," said a voice behind him.

He turned to see who it was, but the man was already a table away. Still, the interruption had been a blessing because it kept Cam from doing something totally stupid. He cleared his throat. What the hell was he doing flirting with Seth's girl? This wasn't a date. This was a chance for him to honor his promise and for his mother to enjoy herself.

"Are you going to ask me to dance again?" Nicole's question ended a long awkward moment between them.

"Would you like me to?" It wasn't a good idea. If only she didn't fit so well in his arms, keeping her at a distance while dancing would be easier.

Her grin was infectious. "I thought that was obvious." And much too hard to ignore.

Taking a quick look around, he tugged on his tie. "There are a ton of other guys here who look like they're dying to take you for a spin." He drew a hand through his hair, then let his arm drop, his fingers resting on the table. "Maybe you should give them a chance, rather than letting me have all the fun."

"I don't want to dance with them." She placed her hand over his. "I want to dance with you."

Warmth pooled where her hand touched, and a spark of heat headed straight to his groin. When she glanced at him like that, he could deny her nothing. What's more, he had no intention of doing so. After all, he rationalized mentally, Seth wouldn't mind him dancing with her because that was what she wanted to do.

This time rather than a fast salsa, the band was playing a slow, sultry song. The second he took her in his arms, Cam knew he was a goner. She fit as if she'd been made for him. A few inches under six feet, he wasn't a big guy, but a daily workout kept him from being a total wimp. Her five-foot-four-inch frame was the perfect height with or without the heels she wore.

While moving in unison to the music, her scent wrapped around him, and when she snuggled in closer, he never wanted the song to end.

Unfortunately, it did, or maybe it had been a good thing, considering the heat of desire now burning inside his gut.

"It's hot in here," he said, pulling at his collar after releasing his hold on Nicole. He needed fresh air and someplace to cool off. Fast.

"There's a courtyard through that doorway." She grabbed his hand and led him through the double doors.

A burst of cool air hit his face and felt good. Fingers still intertwined, he followed her to the edge of what looked to be a balcony overlooking the grounds. When she released his hand, he shoved it and the other one into his pockets. If he hadn't, the consequences for his actions would be dire.

All he could think of while watching her in the moonlight was what it would be like to kiss her. She had flawless skin and beautiful round eyes that seemed to miss nothing.

Finally, she met his gaze. "What was Afghanistan like?"

As if he'd been slapped in the face, the question brought him back to reality and his true mission. Thankfully, it was enough to take his thoughts off of doing something really, really stupid.

"Surreal," he answered honestly.

She sighed and looked at the horizon. Obviously, she was thinking about Seth—another reason to be glad he hadn't kissed her. "I don't even know what really happened when Seth died."

The comment confirmed his suspicion about the direction of her thoughts. "Really?" But it also shocked him. "His parents didn't tell you?" He'd love to rectify the situation, but he remembered Colleen's warning about upsetting her. And upsetting her was the last thing he wanted to do. Especially tonight.

"We weren't close. Seth always said they'd come around after we were married. Now I never see them." The soft laugh she let out held no humor. "We don't exactly run in the same circles."

Cam had never met Seth's parents, but he'd heard enough about them from Seth to realize that they might not have approved of his best man either. He glanced up at the heavens. *I feel for you, buddy*, he said in a quick prayer. Having parents like that would be hard to overcome. Seth was so friendly and outgoing. To know him, you'd never believe the Bakers were worth millions.

And Nicole deserved someone like that. Not someone like him. Someone so jaded that he'd stopped enjoying life.

Until tonight, he realized, unable to discount the fact that he was enjoying himself—too much for his own good. And at twelve o'clock, his princess would disappear.

Chapter 8

As if living in a dream, Nicole took delight in the evening, especially the dancing. Yet from the moment she mentioned Seth, her joy faded. The easy flow of conversation slowed to a trickle of wooden words, on both his part and hers.

If only she knew more about how her fiancé had died, that part of her life could finally be put to rest in her mind. Maybe then her heart would heal.

Somehow she felt closer to Seth when she was with Cam, despite the attraction between them. Every time their eyes met and a thrill went through her, it was like a double-edged sword, slicing her heart in two. One side wanted it to continue forever, and the other wished it would go away.

"Do you miss him?"

Nodding, she didn't need to ask Cam who he meant. "Every day." She offered him a wan smile. "How about you?"

Cam shoved his hands into his pockets, something he'd done many times during the night. "Yeah." He glanced at a point beyond her shoulder before meeting her gaze. "He was the best friend I ever had."

That explained her connection to him. "I'm glad you decided to come tonight," she said in an attempt to return to their earlier camaraderie. "It seems as if we've known each other a long time. I feel comfortable with you."

"You wouldn't say that if you knew of my sins." He refocused on the earlier spot for the longest time before exhaling an audible sigh. "We should go inside." He held out his hand. "It looks like dinner is about to be served, and I'm famished."

Nicole's fingers were engulfed in his warm ones as he guided her toward the door. The entire time they walked, her thoughts were on why she liked him so much when her heart still yearned for Seth. Still, tonight had been a nice diversion from thinking about her loss. She might never find the type of relationship they'd shared together with anyone else, but did that mean she couldn't find comfort with someone new? Someone like Cam? The idea required more thought.

During dinner she studied him. He seldom spoke, listening to others converse about the country's state of affairs. When he did happen to say something, his comments were well-thought out and very polite, even when it was obvious he didn't agree with what had been said.

This would have been Seth's world, just as it was Maggie's, who was more inclined to hobnob with the movers and shakers of the East Bay than Nicole was. And Cam fit right in.

Would it be such a bad thing to have him as a friend? The idea had merit. The more she thought about it as she ate, the more she liked it. One could never have too many friends. Besides, he'd already claimed to be too busy for relationships, so she didn't have to worry about leading him on when so much of her heart belonged to another—even though that person was dead. She wondered if it were even possible for her to love again after surviving her loss.

As dinner wound down, the band switched to playing livelier music.

"I believe this is my dance," Cam said, pushing his chair back from the table.

"I do believe you are correct, kind sir." Grinning, Nicole allowed him to help her rise.

She could dance with him for the rest of the night, she realized as he spun her around the floor. In fact, she did dance with him for a good part of the night.

When the band took a break, she laughed, practically tripping until Cam's strong arms caught her. Somehow, being in his embrace just felt right and she leaned into him, hoping he'd continue holding her.

Nicole must have drunk too much punch, which had been spiked with Kentucky's finest according to Maggie, because she never wanted the evening to end. That thought stopped her and she stiffened.

Cam immediately let go of her. "Sorry. I didn't mean to offend you."

His apologetic tone drew her gaze and she looked up. "You didn't."

Their gazes locked. Something zinged inside her, just as it had those gazillion other times they happened to stare into each other's eyes during the course of the evening. This was not good. What was worse was that he seemed to be fighting their attraction, and she knew she should do the same.

But she didn't want to. For one night, she wanted to forget Seth and the heartache his death had caused. She wanted to be whole again. To laugh again. To see a sunset, and most of all, to find joy again. Yet it seemed ironic that it was one of Seth's friends who made it all possible.

The drive to Nicole's apartment was made with Conchetta chatting in the backseat, recounting all the wonderful aspects of the event. Dreamily, Nicole stared out into the dark night. Her evening had been more than wonderful. It had been enchanting—if not a night to mend a broken heart, then one to begin its healing.

Cam parked and rushed around to open her door.

In silence, he accompanied her inside. The elevator ride seemed to take forever, and Nicole was dying to ask if she'd ever see him again. The thought of him disappearing for good left her feeling a little bereft, which was an incredible improvement over grief and sorrow. Still, she'd rather have the tiny thrills and excitement of the earlier evening to look forward to rather than disappointment.

At her door and with key in hand, she unlocked and opened it before glancing back at him. Cam ran a hand over his face before wrapping it around the back of his neck and rubbing. The movement drew her attention to his face. His expression seemed to mirror her thoughts as he murmured, "I had a nice time tonight."

"So did I," she admitted, sending an invitation with her eyes.

Instead of going inside, she waited in anticipation, holding her head up and praying he'd take her up on it. Not since high school and the first time she'd kissed Seth had she wanted another man's lips on hers. But she would cherish Cam's kiss. The evening wouldn't be complete without it. Finally, his head moved lower and his mouth hovered over hers.

"I shouldn't be doing this," he whispered, grazing back and forth.

The almost-kisses were enough to drive her insane with need.

"But I can't help myself."

And then his lips were there, devouring hers in a kiss that shouldn't have felt so good. But it did, and she wrapped her arms around him in an effort to draw him closer. If he hadn't kissed her when he did, she'd been ready to become the aggressor, which was totally unlike her.

The mindless kiss continued as want and need drove her to open more.

Disappointment swamped her when he broke the kiss and rested his chin on the top of her head. He was breathing as heavily as she was. "Jesus, Nicole, I never meant for that to happen," he said in between breaths, seeming to gain control.

A flush of heat seared her face and she looked past his neck, totally embarrassed at how quickly her thoughts had gotten out of control. "Do you really mean that?" She asked because she really wanted to know. No, she needed to know.

He glanced down at her and nipped her lips, his mouth traveling to her ear. "No. I took what I wanted, but that doesn't make it right."

"What if I wanted it too?"

"Then I'd say we've got a problem." Placing his hand on the small of her back, he gave a slight push. Once she was inside her apartment, he quickly shut the door behind her.

She sank against the cool wood and leaned her head back, listening to his footsteps recede. When silence surrounded her again, Nicole headed for her bedroom. Cam might have thought their kiss was a problem, but she didn't. No. That kiss had given her a sense of freedom from her grief.

THE PROMISE OF TOMORROW

Without knowing it, Cam had given her the promise of tomorrow.

Chapter 9

The next week whizzed by in a blur of activity for Nicole. Which was a good thing, leaving her little time to think about Cam. It was bad enough keeping her emotions under wraps before last weekend. Her mom and Colleen were so used to her mooning over Seth's death. Of course they'd be happy she was moving on. Unfortunately, moving on was so difficult to do. The fact that another man besides Seth was in her thoughts at all should have been a good thing. Irrational or not, she felt guilty.

Wiping off a smudge on a crystal bracelet for a customer, Nicole wondered how it had happened. Obviously, her mother had been right about getting out. Too bad the first guy she "got out" with wasn't interested in a relationship. Or maybe that was the exact reason he'd slipped under her radar. Whatever it was, she wished she'd stayed home last Saturday night. Her feelings were now so jumbled, it was amazing she could function at all.

Nicole finished with the sale. As the customer turned to leave, her cell phone rang. Nicole reached for it and saw an unfamiliar number flash on the small screen.

"Hello," she said after connecting to the call.

"Nicole?"

The accent registered instantly. "Yes, it's me, Conchetta. How are you?"

"I'm fine." There was a hesitation before she added, "I was wondering if you'd like to come to dinner one night here at Windsor Manor." Another pause followed. "As a thank-you for such a wonderful evening."

The invitation seemed like a godsend. Nicole could pick Conchetta's brain about her son. Lightning quick, the thought filled her with guilt. Just a week ago, she'd had no such thoughts.

Thinking them seemed disloyal to Seth's memory somehow. Until Colleen's voice plowed into her musings with common sense. They hadn't been married, and Seth wouldn't want her to stop living. Since her mother had been right about going out, Nicole figured she was probably right about this too.

Having weighed the pros and cons and discarded all the obstacles, she grinned. "Okay, I'd love to. When and where?"

"How about tonight? Say around six thirty?"

"That'll work with my schedule." Heavens, there was no schedule to even check. What did that say about her life? Refusing to dwell on it, she wrote down the instructions and hung up.

Humming, she unlocked a case to set a necklace her previous customer had decided against back inside.

"You seem cheerful all of a sudden," Mary Ann said, coming up behind her carrying a box of jewelry that she'd obviously just created. "Does this have anything to do with the hunk Mom set you up with?"

"Maybe." Ordinarily the comment would rankle, as it was intended, but not today. What pleased her even more was that her answer had piqued Mary Ann's curiosity. Her sister was dying to ask; Nicole could see it in her eyes. Instead of satisfying her nosiness, she relocked the case and moved to the register.

"You'd better be careful." Mary Ann began unloading bracelets one by one onto a bracelet bar.

"Oh, Mar, those are absolutely exquisite." Nicole waited a heartbeat, then succumbed to curiosity herself. "What do you mean, I'd better be careful?"

Mary Ann chuckled. "Mom and Maggie are clearly playing matchmaker again."

Nicole shrugged. "I don't think so. I think they just want me to quit feeling so sad about Seth."

"Yes, well, that too," she agreed. "Still, you may just wake up one morning and find yourself in love."

That isn't about to happen anytime soon. At Mary Ann's arched brow, Nicole said aloud, "He's nice and he's fun. And yes, he's also taken my mind off of Seth, but my heart is still tender. And besides, he's not interested in a relationship."

"Really?" Mary Ann studied her face for a lengthy moment. "Well," she huffed out. "Don't say I never warned you."

Nicole refused to let Mary Ann's comments ruin her good mood. For the rest of the day she stayed busy, but the smile never left her face. She couldn't wait for quitting time. When the thought struck, she realized just how far she'd come in less than a week.

Ordinarily, Nicole dreaded quitting for the day because it meant going home to a lonely apartment. Of course, that had been her doing, and in reality, going home to an empty apartment had been a whole lot better than going home to her mom and dad's house, only to feel as if she wasn't living up to their expectations.

• • •

Cam knocked on his mother's apartment door. About to enter, he started when the door opened and the person who answered wasn't his mother but the same man who had been at his mother's side for most of the gala last Saturday night.

"Come in, come in," Conchetta said from behind him. "Did you meet Anthony?"

"Anthony?" Cam saw immediately why his mom was attracted to the guy. Anthony was very good-looking with a full head of silver hair and an easy smile. He wore pleated slacks and a dress shirt with the sleeves rolled up. Both looked expensive and not off the rack.

"Yes, Anthony Morales. And you must be Roberto." Offering a friendly smile, he held out his hand.

"I go by Cam," he said, shaking the man's hand. Anthony had a firm grip. He also looked at his mother in a way no one else had—at least, not in a long, long time. Suspicion rose up along with the idea that maybe the man was hanging around his mom for nefarious reasons. Cam had read about guys taking advantage of older women, and he didn't want his mother to be one of those women.

"I made eggnog," his mother chimed in. "Have a glass while

we wait for our other guest. Yours doesn't have bourbon."

"Other guest?" Cam lifted the tray off the counter before she could protest and set it on the coffee table. He hurried to help her, but Anthony was already by her side, easing her into her chair before sitting in the one next to her.

Once comfortable, she folded her hands and placed them on her lap. "I'm having a small dinner party in the dining room. I made all the arrangements with the staff." Her expression could only be called animated, just as it had been the other night. "They're holding a table for us."

"Who is this guest? You never said." Cam took a small sip, then a bigger one.

"You'll find out when she gets here."

Cam eyed his mom, whose expression was now closed. "She?" *Ah, a mystery guest*, he thought, gulping another mouthful. "This is good." He held up the glass.

"I'm glad you like it."

His mother was certainly on a roll today. He tossed out a careless smile. "You didn't spike it, did you?"

"Of course I didn't."

"You should try it, though," Anthony said. "The bourbon in it is Woodford Reserve."

"No, thanks." Cam waved it off, not wanting to make a big deal of it in front of her "gentleman caller." Not boyfriend; moms didn't have boyfriends. At least, not his mother. "I'm on call."

One would think after a decade and a half, having to make up an excuse as to why he chose not to drink wouldn't bother him. It shouldn't, but it did. His dad had died on the job because he'd been drunk. There'd been no workmen's compensation because he'd caused the accident. At age fifteen, Cam and an incident involving alcohol had history almost repeating itself, only a generation later. The ensuing car crash spurred the decision to never end up like his dad.

"Besides, I rarely drink."

"Ah, I see," Anthony said, but his expression said otherwise.

The next few minutes ticked by in strained silence.

The doorbell pealed.

"There she is, right on time." Conchetta started to get up, but Anthony placed a hand on her shoulder, stopping her.

Cam had a strong dislike for the guy, but after witnessing that act of kindness toward his mother earlier, his opinion softened a bit. She had a difficult enough time walking and moving about, thanks to severe arthritis in her hips, knees, and shoulders. Movement was supposed to be good for her joints—kind of like lubricating them—but that didn't make it any easier for her.

"Hi. Hope I'm not late."

The feminine voice registered and Cam's heartbeat sped up. He glanced at his mom, tamping down elation as realization set in. This was something she'd set up . . . for him. Her satisfied expression said so.

"Oh no," Conchetta said. "In fact, we're having eggnog before we go down, and you have plenty of time for one."

Cam's mental tug-of-war ensued. Part of him wanted to crawl under the table and hide, while the other part wanted to give his mother a big hug.

"Sounds like a great idea. I love eggnog." Nicole stepped into the room and halted the second her gaze landed on Cam. A surprised expression took over her face. She obviously hadn't expected to see him any more than he'd expected to see her.

Deep down, he knew it wasn't a good idea to spend more time with her. What's more, he couldn't muster up the energy to care, and refused to worry about getting too involved with her tonight.

The memory of their kiss came to the forefront of his thoughts. Judging from the look forming in her eyes, she hadn't forgotten it either.

His mom had invited her. Nicole had come of her own free will, and he planned to do everything in his power to ensure she had a good time.

Cam set his glass aside and jumped up. "I'll get it for you." As Anthony moved to sit beside his mother again, he pointed to the sofa he'd just vacated. "Have a seat."

Twenty minutes later, Nicole finished off the last of the

eggnog and set the glass on the table next to her. "That was delicious."

"Would you like another?" Cam asked, about to rise.

Shaking her head, Nicole placed a hand on his arm, halting him. "If I have another, it'll spoil my appetite. Worse, I won't be able to drive home."

Glancing at the spot where her fingers lingered, Cam almost forgot to breathe as one thought bounced around in his brain. If she couldn't drive, she'd have to spend the night. Conchetta didn't have room, but he did. Then rational thought returned and quashed the idea faster than a catcher's mitt stopped a ball with a *thunk* in the glove.

Conchetta looked at her watch. "We don't have time. They're expecting us downstairs in five minutes."

Relief poured out of Cam as he stood along with the others. As they started for the door, he silently chastised himself for his foolishness and resolved to keep from getting carried away like that for the rest of the evening.

"I should warn you, the average age in the dining room is late sixties," he said in a low voice into Nicole's ear. The topic was as good a diversion as any to control his errant thoughts.

"And you're warning me because ...?" Pausing to allow Anthony and his mother to go well ahead of them, she glanced at him, her gaze curious.

Cam shrugged. "Most people under the age of thirty don't like being around the 'senior crowd,' as my mom calls her friends who live here."

"I'm not like most people my age." She fell into step next to him. "What's more, I like the older generation. They're full of stories about the past and if you listen long enough, you can learn a lot that isn't in any textbook."

"How true. I never thought of it that way." His mother had told him all about Mexico and her family. Life there was hard, and she never took her American citizenship or the opportunity it offered for granted, like so many in this country did. Cam was even guilty of doing so at times.

Cam caught Nicole's quick secret smile, one that made him

question whether she had picked up on his earlier thoughts about having her to himself for the night. Sighing, he kept his gaze straight ahead. The notion divided his emotions. One part intrigued him enough to return the smile, and the other part worried the hell out of him.

• • •

Cam's mother and her boyfriend had gone upstairs to get her shawl. They planned to take in the movie on the second floor. Nicole remained behind with Cam, having already said her good-byes and thanks for a wonderful evening.

Unfortunately, she didn't want the night to end, which was why she hesitated in making her final exit. Cam didn't seem like he was in any big hurry either, so the two lingered in the huge reception hall. In the center was a gigantic tree decorated lavishly. A baby grand piano was at one end of the sitting room, and several oversized sofas and chairs were spread about. Cam led Nicole over to one of the chairs. In an attempt to extend her stay, she sat. He did likewise, sitting close enough so their knees almost touched.

"You looked like you really enjoyed yourself in there."

"Well." She shrugged. "I already told you—"

His laugh cut her off. "That you're not like most. I believe you." The admiration shining in his eyes sent a flush of warmth from her heart all the way to her toes.

"Dinner was interesting," she said, nodding.

"I'll say. You had them talking. Usually, they're a closed-mouth bunch."

"Who wouldn't be if there is no one around to listen?"

"Okay, I'll give you that." He broke off, assessing her with his eyes. "How'd you get to be so intuitive at such a young age?"

Nicole puffed out her chest in mock outrage. "I'll have you know I'll be twenty-seven on my next birthday."

Grinning, he shook his head. "That old, huh?"

She tilted her head at a higher angle in order to peer down her nose at him. "How old are you?"

"Thirty." His grin expanded as he gestured with his hand.

"And you didn't answer my question."

"What question?"

Cam leaned closer, well into her space. "Evading will not work with me."

The cadence of his whispered voice shot through her ears. That, along with his nearness, made her think of things she shouldn't be thinking of . . . like kissing him.

Her focus landed on his lips for a nanosecond, then she chickened out and dropped her gaze to his hands. "I'd say it's worked pretty good so far." God, he even had gorgeous hands. The memory of being in his arms flashed inside her mind's eye before she realized he was speaking. She looked up in the nick of time.

"Really? That's your best answer?" He gave her a no-nonsense look, but rather than release eye contact, he kept a solid hold on it. For much too long.

Nicole swallowed hard, finding it difficult to ignore the intensity of his gaze. Finally, she laughed. "Okay, you win. I'm the baby and because I'm the baby, I got to spend a lot of time with my grandmother. Grandma Murphy loved to tell me stories. Her favorite subject when I was younger was how things were when she was growing up in the US in the late twenties and early thirties, and during World War II." She paused to take in a deep breath.

He made a *go on* signal with his hand.

"I always wondered what it would be like to go without the things we take for granted, like sugar, rubber, and electricity. Not for a day or a week, but for years." She gave him a pointed look. "Did you know the government rationed foodstuffs during the Second World War and had rolling blackouts to conserve energy?"

"Yeah, I remember studying that in school." Grinning, he nodded.

"And during the Great Depression, there was no work for tens of thousands of people."

His amused expression registered. "I read about that too." He was teasing her.

Slightly chagrined, she said, "I know I'm babbling."

He sobered. "No, don't stop. I'm enjoying learning about what interests you."

"I just find that time so interesting." Shrugging, she stared at him, now noting only sincerity in his expression. "People were tougher back then. They had to be with no safety net like welfare or Social Security. Men, with families to provide for, used to come up to my grandmother's back door to ask for work. They didn't want charity. Her mother would have them wash windows or rake leaves for the food she had to give them or the extra money she had. No one of that ilk would take a handout." She snorted. "Things have sure changed."

"Your story reminds me of the men at the rehab center. They don't want handouts. They want to work. Yet to work, they have to get better. They deserve more than Uncle Sam has provided, that's for damn sure."

Stunned, she drew back in her chair. "You didn't tell me you work at a rehab center."

"I don't work there, I'm a volunteer."

"Wow. That must be wonderful to help your fellow soldier. Tell me about your volunteering."

Cam cleared his throat and looked down, suddenly appearing uncomfortable. "It's nothing. I work with vets who've lost limbs or have some issues with overcoming PTSD."

When she tried to get him to elaborate, he answered her questions with either yes, no, or other one-worded answers. Finally, she switched tactics and said, "I'm glad your mother asked me to dinner tonight."

"Yeah." His smile didn't reach his eyes when he nodded, which tended to negate the gesture and his answer.

Their earlier camaraderie had dissipated.

"It's getting late." She rubbed her arms and stood. The awkward silence was cue enough. "I guess I should go."

He jumped up, clearly relieved. "I'll walk you to your car." Whether it was due to having the conversation steered away from him, or that he was finally going to be rid of her, she didn't know.

Chapter 10

As Cam trailed Nicole out to the parking lot, he did a quick surveillance of the area—mostly out of habit after Afghanistan. Things were quiet, as usual. The facility skirted a crime-ridden area, but the security cameras kept the criminal element away.

Nicole looked around. There was only one car parked in the lot provided for visitors, and it was obviously hers. "Where's your car?"

"I walked." He shoved his hands into his pockets and started toward the cute little Mazda that suited her.

"You walked?" She took more notice of her surroundings. "You're kidding."

Cam's gaze followed hers. There were no residential areas within sight. Maybe it was time he let her in on who he really was. "I don't own a car."

He noted a bit of confusion in her gaze, but once it cleared there was only curiosity. Not scorn or censure or whatever else he'd expected. A lot of Silicon Valley women wouldn't give him the time of day if they knew of his car-less status. "I don't live far."

"Want a lift?"

Hell yes, he wanted a lift. The question held all he could hope for—acceptance, encouragement, friendship, a prelude to more. But she had to know he wasn't the right guy for her.

"Why are you offering?" A need to hear the answer drove him to ask the question, even though the answer might be something he should avoid at all costs.

"Because I enjoy your company, and I'd like to get to know you better."

"What if you don't like what you find out?" He frowned. "I'd rather not destroy what's already been built."

"I bet you say that to all the girls." She tucked her arm in his as they continued walking toward her car.

"Only the ones I want to get to know better," he said, unable to stop the words from spilling out.

"So, that means you like me too, right?"

He laughed, enjoying their banter. No wonder Seth had been smitten. The more Cam was with her, the more he wanted to be with her. In fact, he'd begun telling himself that by being around her, he was honoring his promise. Whether it was true or not no longer mattered. At this point, Cam couldn't stop the rising tide of his feelings toward her. "Come home with me?"

Damn, the minute the question burst forth, he stopped short, regretting asking it. His common sense continually had trouble surging through the testosterone overload he'd experienced since first landing eyes on her. "Forget I asked. It's not a good idea."

"Shush." She placed her fingers over his lips. "Don't say that."

Her touch was electric. More than anything, he wanted to nip at her fingertips. Instead he met her gaze, not bothering to hide the intense emotions she awakened in him. Emotions he had no idea were buried deep inside his soul.

She swallowed hard but didn't flinch. He watched with disbelieving eyes as her smile turned sultry, and that hand moved to slink around his neck. In slow motion, she raised up on tiptoes, her lips moving toward his while using her hand to help guide him.

As if he needed an invitation to kiss her. Hell, he'd thought of nothing else since the last time ... had even dreamed of kissing her again. Reality was so much better than his dreams. She tasted like honey, and like the starving man he was, he wanted to drink all he could. He pressed her against the car's door frame. Unable to stop his hands from touching her waist, and then moving higher to the underside of her breasts, he groaned and kept his mouth moving.

Stop, his inner voice cautioned. But he was too far under her spell to heed the warning. Instead, he nipped his way to her ears.

"I want you. I know I'm a pale replacement for Seth, but I can't help wanting you."

When she stiffened under his hands, he loosened his hold and looked at her.

Nicole leaned away, her expression horrified. "I'm sorry. I don't know what I was thinking."

Mistake or not, he refused to back down. "How about that you feel the same." She'd been into the kiss as much as him. Hell, she'd started it.

"Of course I feel the same." She pushed at his chest. "That's the frickin' problem."

Cam released his hold but didn't move away. "How is that a problem?"

"You know as well as I do, since you were the one to point it out." Nicole wouldn't meet his gaze.

A burst of frustration rose up, morphing into anger in a heartbeat. "Seth is dead," he said, lashing out.

"I know that," she shot back just as loudly.

When he spied the hurt in her expression, his anger evaporated. His stance softened, and he gentled his tone. "He's not coming back."

"I know that too." She stepped out of his reach and began to pace. "I guess I'm just not ready for a guy like you."

And because he wanted to be the kind of guy she'd indicated, he could only say, "I'm here. And I'm definitely sticking around awhile." Where Nicole was concerned, he suddenly realized he could wait a lifetime and still have the patience to wait longer.

"Yeah, I sort of figured that out too." She wrapped her fingers around his sleeve and pressed her face against his chest.

Damn it all. Curling his hands into fists to keep from disturbing this newfound trust, he swallowed hard. What did he do now?

"I don't want to be alone tonight." When she looked up, her forlorn expression tore at his insides.

"Me neither." He gripped her shoulders. "Come home with me. No strings. Just comfort." As he spoke, another realization hit. He meant every word.

When she nodded, the knot inside his chest loosened a bit. Damn, how had this tiny speck of a girl gotten under his skin so quickly?

"The guys at the station are hosting a Christmas party for the kids in the neighborhood tomorrow." He spoke rapidly in an effort to ease the fist clutching his insides. "Some of them won't see many presents under the tree, if they even have one, other than what we give them."

"I'd love to tag along." Relief rang high in her voice, striking another of his heartstrings.

As foolish as it was to make future plans, he decided, so what? It was only a Christmas party. What could go wrong? "Let's walk. It's a beautiful night."

"Okay." She grabbed his hand, interlacing fingers, and began swinging their arms in a cadence that matched their steps. It felt so natural to be walking beside her like this—as though they'd done it a million times.

After a block, her soft voice rent the air. "Can I let you in on a secret?" She stopped and sent him an apprehensive glance.

Nodding, he offered an encouraging smile. "Sure."

She inhaled deeply, as if what she was about to say wasn't easy.

"Go on," he urged, when she hesitated a few more seconds. To make it easier, he started walking again.

"Christmas is only a few days away, and already some of the dread I've felt over surviving it is dissipating." She squeezed his hand and his heart soared. "I used to be a kindergarten teacher. I used to love kids, and loved to be around them." She paused, took another deep breath, and continued. "After Seth died, I couldn't do it anymore. Children are no longer in my future."

"That's sad," he murmured. He could picture her with a half dozen kids around her feet. His kids. He snorted mentally. Yeah, what the hell was he smoking? The thought was a pipe dream, to be sure.

Suddenly car tires screeched a half block away. Cam stiffened. Even after a year of being away from Afghanistan, sudden sounds still had the ability to elicit a reflexive response. His attention shifted in the direction of the noise.

A speeding car came around the corner, careened out of control, and finally hit an oncoming bus. Cam shook off his initial reaction. He was in San Jose, not a war zone. The thought allowed him to focus on the accident in front of him.

His training fully kicking in, Cam ran to the bus as it was closer and did a visual assessment of the situation. The bus driver was dazed, but unhurt. Thankfully, the car's impact had done little damage to the front of the bus. There were three passengers, all of whom had been tossed about during the crash. He was able to get them out. A quick check revealed none had serious injuries.

Cam then concentrated on the car. As he rushed toward the vehicle, it suddenly burst into flames. *Oh God*, he thought, staving off memories of the last time he'd come so close to burning wreckage. The driver was still inside and unconscious. Cam had to get him out.

Working at warp speed, he yanked the front passenger door open, the door farther away from the flames. It took some finagling to unsnap him from the seat belt and untangle him from the air bag. When the man was finally free, Cam was able to pull him to safety. Running, half dragging and half carrying the guy, he was barely clear of the car before it exploded in a fiery boom. The force of the blast knocked him to the ground.

The past merged with the present as more memories from that horrible day flashed, refusing to be vanquished. He was living the nightmare all over again.

At that point, Cam wasn't sure what was real any longer. He looked down at the man in his arms and saw Seth, bleeding from fatal wounds. "It's okay," he whispered over and over, rocking him.

"Cam!" When Nicole's voice calling his name penetrated his thoughts, he glanced up. It took a moment to realize where he was and what he'd done. He blinked back tears and wiped moisture off his face. *Shit*. He wasn't in Afghanistan, and the old man whose head was still in his lap wasn't Seth. Would Cam ever be free from his guilt over that fateful day? He finally realized that what had happened wasn't his fault, any more than he was responsible for the stranger now lying in his arms.

Shaking free of the nightmare, he let go of the man and prayed he hadn't caused any spinal injuries. The guy was barely breathing.

Sirens in the distance got closer by the second. When the EMTs arrived, he recognized two men he worked with on a daily basis. John Wilson and Jordan Scott.

"What happened?" Wilson asked, kneeling next to Cam as he took over.

Relieved, Cam stood. "Heart attack or some kind of seizure is my guess." He went on to explain that there was no alcohol on the man's breath, and he didn't look the sort to do crack or heroin like a high percentage of the patients on their calls did.

Scotty placed him on a backboard. "We'll take it from here." Wilson placed an oxygen mask over his mouth and started an IV.

"I hope I didn't mess up his spine by pulling him out of the car like I did."

Wilson looked over at the burning wreckage. "You either had to pull him out or he'd be toast right now."

Cam nodded and turned to the police officer who'd arrived and was taking statements.

Now that the ordeal was pretty much over, he just wanted to go home. Alone. That was when he remembered his companion. What must Nicole have thought of his earlier outburst? This situation was a perfect example of why it was better to be alone and unencumbered. Any more flare-ups would surely lead to questions about his past. An urge to get the hell out of here unnoticed was all encompassing.

"What?" Nicole asked when he stared at her a little too long.

"Nothing." The world began closing in on him. If he didn't get out of here, he'd lose what little control he had left. He started walking toward his house.

"Oh no, you can't shut me out now." She pulled on his sleeve with enough force to get him to stop.

He turned to her. "What do you want me to say? That I'm fine?" He grunted. "Well, I'm not fine. The goddamned war that

Americans had no business being in has messed with my head." He scrubbed a hand over his face and met her gaze. "Okay? My best friend died in my arms and . . ." Oh God, if he didn't shut up, he'd be telling her everything. Then she'd really hate him.

"It's okay."

"It'll never be okay. I've lost too much," he admitted, allowing his shoulders to slump.

That seemed to make her angry, and she shoved him. "You think you're the only one to lose someone you loved from a senseless war?" Tears made her eyes stand out in the dark.

Suddenly Cam felt ashamed for lashing out at her. She'd lost just as much as him. Maybe more, since her future had been tied to Seth. After all, she was living proof of what became of a woman whose dream of having children with the love of her life had been obliterated with one IED.

Christ, life was mixed up. If only Seth had lived and Cam could have taken his place, the universe would be a better place. At least the woman who was coming to mean more to him than he cared to admit would still have a chance to fulfill her dream with a half dozen of Seth's kids.

"I'm sorry." He drew a hand through his hair, struggling to regain his equilibrium. "You're right." He turned. "I should probably walk you back to your car."

Again, she grabbed at his arm to stop him. "No way, Jose."

"The name's Roberto, not Jose."

Nicole straightened to her full height. "No way, Roberto." The formidable expression that settled over her face was all too familiar. "So what was that all about back there?" When he remained mute, she added, "Okay, you don't want to talk about it, we won't." She hesitated. "But you need me tonight." Her expression and tone of voice said he should just get used to the idea, because she wasn't budging.

Cam blinked away a bit of moisture that had formed in his eyes. Had to be allergies because men like him didn't cry. Or they seldom cried, he amended, remembering Seth's death.

Why did death and dying have to permeate his life? Why couldn't he be normal? Why couldn't he have Nicole? So many whys, yet only one answer. Because this was the way God had intended for Cam's life to go.

Still, he couldn't deny the naked truth. "I do need you. I'd be much obliged if you stayed. I can sleep on the couch."

Again, she shook her head. "You'll sleep on the bed and I'll keep you company."

"I don't know if that's any better." When she gave him an odd look, he realized he'd spoken out loud. She cuffed his shoulder playfully. "What?" he said. "It'll be torture."

"Now that's the Cam I've come to know and love."

Her smile could light up an entire block, but he was satisfied with just having her light up his life for a while. He refused to think about her use of the L-word. She was just trying to cheer him up. "Come on. Let's go." He slung an arm around her and headed in the direction of his apartment.

As long as she was with him, the light in his heart would stay on. The time would come when she'd realize that he didn't deserve her, and she'd move on to someone who did. Until then, he'd be warm and content. So what if they never made love? Making love to Seth's Nicole seemed like a sacrilege anyway.

Finally home, he opened the door and pushed it aside to let her go in ahead of him.

"Wow, this is nice."

He looked around and tried to see it through her eyes. It was nice, except it was pretty bare. He shrugged. "I know the landlord, and do some maintenance here and there for a break on the rent."

"And you don't have a car."

"I plan to wait until I graduate to take on that expense." He then explained about paying for the balance of his mother's assisted-living expenses that her Social Security Disability payments didn't cover. His share was a little more than half of her studio apartment at Windsor Manor where the staff took care of her. Cam was grateful for their care when he'd been deployed.

He told Nicole as much as he entered the kitchen, leaving out the part about how his antics during his teens had been a primary reason his mom needed the care in the first place.

"I guess you're not hungry?" He opened the fridge, which was practically as bare as his apartment.

She groaned and rubbed her tummy. "After that dinner?"

"It was filling, wasn't it?" He pulled out two bottled waters and handed her one.

"Well, when the ladies have a distinct desire to please one said customer, he certainly won't starve."

Cam laughed. "Guilty as charged." The waiters and waitresses were mostly college students. "I admit to flirting with a couple of the coeds. A few nice words go a long way to ensuring my mom will receive extra attention during meals."

Her light laugh zinged right through him. If he lived to be a hundred, he doubted he'd ever tire of the sound.

He glanced at his watch, noting it was only nine thirty. "It's still kind of early. Would you like to watch TV? Or find a movie on cable?"

"TV sounds good," she said, poking into his cabinets one by one before she started on the other side of the kitchen.

"If you'd like, I'd be happy to give you a tour that includes opening the drawers too."

She had the decency to blush. "Sorry. My curiosity got the better of me." Her smile was quick. "You'd be surprised what kind of secrets I can uncover just by poking around."

"That's a bad habit."

"Says who?"

"Says me," he said, striding up to her. As he walked, he held eye contact. When she started to move backward, he nodded. "Just remember nosiness has consequences."

"I stand warned." Then her expression turned more serious. "Where's your bedroom?"

Stunned, he took a step back. "Whoa! Watching TV in the bedroom isn't a good idea."

"Get your mind out of the gutter, Cam." She brushed past him. "Let's skip TV. I'm beat." At the hallway, she stopped and turned back. "If I'm spending the night, I'm ready to hit the hay."

Cam moved to show her to his room. "Did you mean it when you said you didn't want me on the couch?" At his bedroom door, he halted and noted that she'd followed. "I'll understand if you say no."

"Silly boy!" Nicole patted his face. "You don't get rid of me that easily."

"I'll get you an extra toothbrush, and you can wear one of my T-shirts and a pair of sweats if you'd like." He found the promised toothbrush and held it out.

"Thanks," she murmured, reaching for it before heading into the bathroom, only to emerge minutes later looking like an angel. Her hair was free from the ponytail and fell around her shoulders. She'd taken off her makeup. Her skin glowed. She looked at him with the question in her eyes.

When he didn't respond, she said, "You mentioned a T-shirt and sweats?"

He searched through his drawers, pulled out a pair of sweatpants along with an old Giants T-shirt a friend had given him, and handed them over for her inspection.

After looking at them, she smiled. "They're perfect." She did an about-face and returned to the bathroom. The door opened within thirty seconds, and she stepped out wearing sweats and a T-shirt that looked much better on her than him.

Cam wondered at the craziness of having to lie next to her all night and not touch her. Still, he'd promised. And one thing he was quickly learning about himself. He wasn't one to go back on his word. If he were, she wouldn't be here tormenting him in the first place.

He slipped into the bathroom to brush his teeth and ready himself for bed. As he spit out the last of the toothpaste, he caught his reflection in the mirror.

Studying his face, he totally decided he'd lost his fricking mind. Seth's Nicole should not be sleeping in his bed. He looked up at the ceiling. *I'm trying, buddy, but she's not making it easy.*

Seth should be the one climbing into bed with Nicole. There was no way he'd ever make a good substitute for his friend. Why Cam had even thought he could was laughable.

With those thoughts, he switched off the light and left the bathroom, only to find Nicole sound asleep in his big bed.

Damn. This was too much. He wanted to hold her and keep her from harm. The only way to do that was to leave her alone. He grabbed a pillow and a spare blanket, and hightailed it to the living room.

Chapter 11

Humming Christmas carols, Nicole moved about, putting the finishing touches on the decorations for the party at the fire station. Only guys were on duty today—guys who knew nothing about decorating for a party—and in Nicole's mind, they had definitely needed some guidance.

"Thanks," one of Cam's coworkers said. Mike, if she remembered correctly. "Now all we need to do is finish wrapping the gifts."

Cam, his arms filled to overflowing with boxes of toys, set them on a table that held festive red and green paper, tape, and bows. "I didn't realize how many there were."

"It won't take long." Nicole picked up one of the wrapping paper rolls. "I'm a pro at wrapping fast. You have to be fast when you have eight nosy brothers and sisters."

She glanced at Cam, who was walking away. "You're not going to help?"

"Mike's on wrapping duty. I'm hanging garlands—as per your demand."

Frowning, she undid the roll. As she cut, she couldn't shake the notion that he was distancing himself from her. An idea that started to form from the moment she'd awakened alone, only to realize that Cam had spent the night on his couch.

When done wrapping several toys, she set them aside. She let her gaze wander toward Cam, who climbed up a ladder to hang the last of the garlands. While watching him work, she tried to figure him out.

Roberto Camareno had deep hurts, probably more hurts than she was holding on to. More than anything, she wanted to unearth them. Bring them out in the light of day and quash them so he'd be pain-free. Thinking of her own pain, she wondered if it were truly possible to extinguish it totally. As much as it had diminished over the last week, there was still a dull ache of longing left behind. The good news for her was that she could now manage to smile in spite of it.

Nicole had Cam to thank for that, which was why the idea of helping him wouldn't dissipate no matter how much he avoided her.

During the next hour, she did everything in her power to be near him. Yet every time she got too close, he'd make up some lame excuse and would deftly dodge her attempts.

When the party began, several dozen noisy kids raced around, too excited to wait for Santa's arrival. Nicole found herself chasing after them and keeping them out of mischief. Thoughts of helping Cam were shoved to the back burner. She'd figure out something later, when she wasn't wiping up spilled juice or sweeping up cheese snack crumbs.

"Who wants to hear a Christmas story," she yelled into the crowd.

Instantly, thirty heads turned her way. That was the beauty of children, she thought, grinning at their cherubic faces. They all had a thirst for stories that a hard life beat out of them as they got older. But no child under the age of seven, as the majority of these kids were, could resist a Christmas story. It was probably why the networks kept running those stupid Rudolph and Frosty the Snowman cartoons during prime time between Thanksgiving and Christmas every year.

"If you sit quietly around the tree, I'll tell you one." She paused, her gaze sweeping over each and every child. "And by the time I'm done, Santa should make an appearance."

• • •

Earlier, Cam had watched Nicole gather up the kids faster than the Pied Piper could take them out of Hamelin. Solid admiration had filled him. She really did know how to deal with kids on their level. From the moment she began the story about a boy who wanted a baseball bat for Christmas, she had them listening to her every word.

He wasn't the only man to notice her skill either. Every guy in the unit gazed at her like she'd hung the moon.

Groveling bunch of idiots . . . what did she see in them?

Gritting his teeth, Cam turned his back on the scene, unwilling to watch any longer. He should be glad that she found other guys interesting enough to joke around with, but it was still hard to watch.

Wilson had it worse than the others. Every time Cam had looked for Nicole, the guy was right there offering her food or drink or sharing a laugh. Wilson was an upstanding guy, someone good enough to take Seth's place. He'd make a much better husband and father than Cam ever could. Nicole deserved someone like Wilson.

Cam wanted the best for Nicole. Didn't he? Of course he did, but he didn't have to watch. He damn sure didn't like the green-eyed monster eating a hole in his gut.

When it seemed that no one would miss him, he slipped out. Nicole was in good hands with Wilson. As much as it hurt to admit it, he knew it was the best for everyone.

He walked the short distance to his apartment. Halfway there, he looked up at the heavens. "Well, good buddy," he said under his breath. "She's on her way to being happy."

If that were true, then why did he feel so bad?

• • •

Laughing at something John said, Nicole looked past his shoulder. *Darn*. She couldn't find Cam in the crowd. Where had he disappeared to? Had he left? And if so, why hadn't he had the decency to say good-bye? Her festive mood plummeted lower than the ground she walked on.

"Hey, Wilson, quit hogging the lady." Jordan Scott, or Scotty, as everyone called him, clapped John on the back. "I think you pissed Cam off. He's gone."

"You're sure?" Nicole glanced at him.

A lump the size of a grapefruit lodged in her throat when he nodded. "Yeah, I saw him head out a few minutes ago."

Somehow she got through the next hour. Unfortunately, her sour mood had affected everyone around her, including John Wilson, an idea substantiated when the guys in Cam's unit began steering clear of her in the last fifteen minutes. Even the kids started avoiding her.

At this point, her presence was a hindrance rather than a help. As Cam had done earlier, she sneaked out.

The fight to keep tears from her eyes was Nicole's biggest obstacle on the drive home.

"Stupid man," she murmured, pulling into a spot near her apartment. As she climbed the stairs, her heart felt heavy. She should be glad to realize her heart hadn't been irrevocably broken after all, but she wasn't. Seth's death was still a painful memory, if one that was slowly fading. This ache was different. Probably because it was fresh.

No matter. She opened her apartment door and stepped inside, letting it slam behind her. As she glanced around, the place appeared empty. Just like her heart.

Chapter 12

"It's Christmas Eve," Mary Ann said, coming up behind Nicole as she finished waiting on a man looking for a last-minute gift for his girlfriend. "You should be spending time with your hunk."

Nicole smiled, then shook her head. "He's not my hunk." He'd never been her hunk, and what's more, he never would be. But she refrained from adding the sentiments.

"Sooo, something must've happened between you two. Of course." She plunked the palm of her hand on her forehead. "No wonder you've been moping around like a slug."

Miffed, Nicole placed her hands on her hips. "I haven't been moping around like a slug."

"Yes, you have." Mary Ann straightened a case with jewelry strewn about due to an earlier rush of guys who'd waited until Christmas Eve to buy for their significant others. "I'd have mentioned it earlier, but I thought maybe it was because of—" She broke off, then cleared her throat. "Because of Seth, and the fact that tomorrow is the anniversary of his death."

Mary Ann pulled up a stool and reached for her hand as she sat. "Want to talk about it?"

"Not really." Nicole sighed and plopped down next to Mary Ann, laying her head against her arm. "Maybe." She smiled when she felt her sister's arm lift and wrap around her shoulders.

"I'm sorry, sis," Mary Ann said, giving her a quick squeeze. "You've sure had a bad year."

"It was starting to get better."

"Because of Cam?"

"Yep."

"Then why is he suddenly out of the picture?"

"He wants to be."

Mary Ann laughed. "Sell me something else. I saw the way he looked at you during the gala last week."

Nicole spent a few minutes bringing Mary Ann up to speed on all that had taken place since then. "Now do you see why I'm so upset? He left me without even saying good-bye."

"Wait." Her sister put up a hand. "Something's off here. No guy with the kind of yearning I glimpsed in his eyes is going to do something like that without a reason."

"He doesn't want to get involved. Isn't that reason enough?"

"What were you doing when he left?"

"I was trying to enjoy myself with his coworkers." She'd gone to extra lengths to meet each and every one.

"And this John Wilson you were telling me about? Was he flirting with you?"

"I wouldn't call it flirting exactly." Suddenly it hit her. "Oh my God. Maybe he was." She closed her eyes and groaned. "I guess I've been out of the dating game too long to recognize it for what it was. I thought he was just being nice." Heck, she'd never been in it to begin with as an adult, so it was an honest mistake. "What do I do now?"

"I can tell you what I'd do, but you may not like hearing it."

"What?"

"If it was me, and I really wanted something, I'd go after it. You're no different." Mary Ann held her gaze. "You have to decide what you want. If it's him, then go get him."

Her sister's advice rolled around in Nicole's brain, stirring up hope. Could she do it? Was the prize worth the chance of rejection? "It can't be that easy, can it?"

"Nothing stopped you from going after Seth when he thought he was too old for you in high school. Or have you forgotten that?"

Seth had been a sophomore at the junior college while she'd just started her senior year of high school. According to him, the years might as well have been decades. Yet, as Nicole's sister just said, his objections had only increased her tenacity.

Maybe she could go after Cam. Then she remembered his reaction the night of the accident. Something was definitely going on deep down inside his soul that needed healing. Did she have the strength to endure what that could entail? Lord, she hoped so. But rather than deal in maybes, she set up a plan to get his attention. Then her no-holds-barred attack would begin.

And what better time to begin her siege than on Christmas Eve?

• • •

Cam placed his elbows on his knees, leaned forward, and stared at the portable fireplace with its fake flames his mother had given him for Christmas. What in the hell had she been thinking when she bought it? And why had she used the little bit of money she had on a gift for him in the first place?

Still, the electric flames did have a mesmerizing effect that helped ease a bruised ego. He'd gotten the day off a while ago in order to spend it with his mother. Unfortunately, she'd called and begged off, saying she was going to the senior crowd's Christmas party with Anthony. Cam was welcome to join them and to bring Nicole. He hadn't had the heart to tell her that he'd pushed Nicole out of his life.

Why spoil her Christmas? Letting his mother think things were great was one of the best gifts he could give her when her main goal in life was to make sure her son had what he needed. Just as it had become Cam's goal to return the favor. After all, she'd sacrificed too much for him already.

It concerned him that she was spending a lot of time with this Anthony guy. What did she really know about him, anyway? And what were the man's intentions toward his mom? Cam planned to find out, but not tonight.

As he glanced around the room, his sense of gloom and doom prevailed. What a dismal way to spend Christmas Eve. Cam quit going to church long before Seth died, so midnight mass was out. The fire station seemed his best option.

Having made the decision, he jumped up, grabbed his jacket, and was out on the street a minute later.

"Hey, Cam," Scotty said when he shoved through the front door of the station. "I thought you'd be with that pretty angel you brought to the Christmas party."

"No. She had plans." With Wilson, most likely. Unable to hold his curiosity at bay, he glanced around. "Where is everybody?"

"It's been unusually slow. Miller is in the back room doing push-ups, and Yeager is sleeping."

"What about Wilson?" The answer would probably hurt like vinegar on a wound, but Cam had to know.

"He drove to Sacramento to be with his family for Christmas. I think it bummed him out to realize that as long as Nicole had the hots for you, he'd never stand a chance."

"No way." Even as relief swamped him, he shook his head. "I thought for sure she was into him."

Scotty's gaze narrowed as he scrutinized Cam's face. "You're a dumbass, man."

Cam's lips twisted into a semblance of a careless grin. "What'd I do?"

"If you can't figure it out, you're more messed up than I thought." Scotty smirked.

"I'm not right for her."

"Nicole didn't look stupid to me. You should let her be the judge of what's right for her."

"I got baggage that'll only weigh her down." Damn, he hadn't admitted that to another breathing soul, and here he was pouring his guts out to Scotty. Maybe he was a dumbass.

"We all got baggage, even Nicole." His friend leaned closer. "I'll let you in on a little secret. Most guys, me included, would cut off his right nut to have a chance at a woman like your Nicole, baggage or no baggage." Scotty threw out a disgusted look and waved a hand. "Now get out of here and go find her. It's Christmas Eve, for Chrisssake."

Could it be that simple? Scotty obviously thought so, and maybe Cam should too. Attaining the guy's permission gave him hope. He might as well admit that he wanted to at least try. "Thanks, man. I owe you."

"No, you paid your dues in Afghanistan. Let's just call it even, though your sacrifice outstrips anything I could do or say at this point."

As Cam started for the door, Scotty yelled, "And Merry Christmas."

Cam spun around, strode up to him with purpose, and hugged him, much to Scotty's chagrin. "Merry Christmas." Grinning, he left to find Nicole, pleased as all get-out that he'd actually done something to leave his coworker speechless.

Cam walked at a brisk pace, reaching for his cell phone, then stuck it back in his pocket. He'd rather not be distracted with walking while talking. Damn, he hoped it wouldn't be too late. Had she made plans for tonight with her family? When he turned the corner, his apartment complex was in sight, and so was a dark blue Mazda in the parking lot. His spirits rose as he picked up speed, going the rest of the distance at a quick jog.

He spotted her before she saw him, and his heart lurched. She sat on the stoop to his unit.

"Hey, stranger," he said, coming up to her and giving her foot a playful nudge.

"Hey, yourself." Her smile could light a dozen Christmas trees. It certainly lit his heart. Then all too quick, a sad expression replaced her smile. "Why'd you leave?"

He didn't have to be clairvoyant to know that she was talking about last Saturday. Shrugging, he held up his hands as if to say he was clueless, which he was. "According to Scotty, it's because I'm a dumbass. I'm inclined to agree with that assessment."

Her smile was back. Maybe not as bright as a moment ago, but it was a definite improvement. "I don't think you're a dumbass."

"Oh?"

"No." Nicole shifted her gaze higher. "I think you're scared."

He swallowed hard and struggled to keep eye contact. If she knew him that well already, God only knew what she'd uncover in a matter of days. Still, he was bent on seeing this through. Let her have the choice and live with the consequences. While helping her to her feet, he prayed it wouldn't be a mistake.

Side by side, they walked into the building and up to his apartment. Cam's hands were damp. He kept having to wipe them on his jeans in efforts to keep them dry. Otherwise, the moment he touched her, she'd figure out how nervous he was.

Her eyebrow arched when he unlocked the door, pushed it open, and said, "Welcome." *Lame, lame, lame.* But he couldn't think of anything better because the sight of her in the living room's light, *his living room*, set his heart pounding. His mind was already a jumbled mess, which coincided with his sweaty palms and did nothing to ease his discomfort.

When he just stood there staring, not bothering to close the front door, she used her foot to kick it shut.

"Okay, you got me. I was scared." He closed his eyes and breathed in her scent. Lord, he was still scared and admitted as much in a burst of honesty. "Petrified would be a better word." When he opened his eyes, the acceptance in her expression nearly did him in. There was a touch of love in her gaze. *Please let it be directed at me.* He really wanted to be the recipient of her love, no matter that he wasn't worthy.

Of their own volition, his arms opened wide. He exhaled the breath he'd held when she stepped into them. "I'm sorry I screwed up."

Nicole put her hand on his lips, the act reminding him of the last time they'd kissed. The desire to kiss her again was so strong, it practically paralyzed Cam. The need must have shown on his face or in his eyes, because she didn't hesitate to rise up on tiptoes, wrap those warm hands around his neck, and pull his head lower.

And when their lips met, he had a good idea what heaven must be like. Nicole's touch soothed his troubled soul. How long it might last, he had no clue. All he knew was that tonight, on this Christmas Eve, they would share something special. Just because they were together.

Eventually, he broke the kiss and leaned back. "I don't have much by the way of food. I was planning on eating with the senior crowd tonight . . . and tomorrow," he admitted with a wry grin, but inside he was groaning. Pretty damned pathetic, now that he thought about it. Maybe it was good that his mom was enjoying people her own age. The same could be said for him, considering he'd much rather spend the evening with Nicole than flirt with the college girls working there who didn't interest him.

"How about we go grocery shopping?"

He threw her a skeptical look. "On Christmas Eve?"

She pulled out her cell phone and started typing. "I'm sure there's someplace open." After spending several minutes searching, she threw out an exasperated huff. "Nothing, unless we want to drive half an hour. Can you believe it? In our commercialized world, there's not much open after six on Christmas Eve but bars and bowling alleys."

"And why is that a bad thing?"

"Because I'm hungry." She began pacing.

"Stop." He grabbed her shoulders to keep her from taking another step. "You're making me dizzy."

She crossed her arms and lifted her shoulders. "Sorry. I was thinking."

His grin was quick. "Do you do that a lot?"

"What? Think?" she asked.

"No, pace."

"Yes."

"So that's how you stay in shape."

She gave an audible snort. "Hardly." Her pacing continued. "I got the matronly genes, in case you haven't noticed."

"What's wrong with that?" He looked her up and down. "More women should look like you."

She stopped short and beamed, making a glow stick come to mind. "Thank you." One that quickly dimmed. "I think." She tucked a strand of hair that had come loose from her ponytail behind her ear and took a few more steps. Suddenly, she spun around. "I have it."

Reaching for her cell phone again, she pressed a few buttons and put the device next to her ear. "Mom? Set two more places." She paused to listen. "Yes, this means we'll be attending midnight mass with you all."

"Wait," Cam practically yelled, shaking his head. This was getting out of hand. Christmas Eve spent quietly in his apartment with Nicole was one thing, but being around a rowdy family where he'd be the outsider was another thing entirely. A root canal sounded more appealing.

She glanced at him, her big brown eyes pleading, and he froze. *Damn.* When she looked at him like that, he realized denying her anything wasn't as simple as saying no.

"Give us about half an hour and we'll be there." She paused. "Love you too." Then she hung up. Shrugging, she smiled apologetically. "At least we'll have food. Besides, you'll love my family."

"I don't feel comfortable around big families." At sleepovers with friends during his early teens, he was usually the kid the moms pitied. Hell, he'd pity any scrawny kid wearing ill-fitting clothes like the one he'd been.

"Why?" Her brow furrowed. "You like my mom, right?"

He nodded. Colleen wasn't like those other women.

"And Mary Ann and her husband, Kyle?" When he nodded a second time, her eyebrows shot up as if to say, *So? What's the problem?*

"It's a throwback from my childhood," he said. When her expression didn't change, he sighed. Might as well let her know in advance that being poor was a shitty way to grow up. "My mother used to clean houses, and her clients used to give us their children's hand-me-downs. I wore them whether they fit or not. Otherwise Mom would have had to spend her hard-earned money unnecessarily." It always drove home the point that he was different. Plus, more often than not he'd been the butt of jokes, not to mention someone for the bullies to target.

"Jeez, Cam. That's so sad. I can't imagine how that felt."

His back went ramrod as he threw his shoulders back. "I don't need your pity."

"Not pity. Understanding and empathy. I used to teach kids who were in the same situation, and I saw firsthand how taunts and being singled out because they were different affected them."

"So, you'll call your mom back and cancel?"

"No. You'll just have to make do and get over it."

Stunned, he could only stare at her. "Excuse me?" She said that so matter-of-factly that Cam wasn't sure how to respond.

"I said—"

"I heard what you said." He scrubbed at his face, still trying to get a handle on the situation. "And what if I don't want to go to midnight mass?"

"Well, that's too bad, because I do." Hands on hips, she frowned. "You can either sit here and wallow in your pitiful childhood memories, or you can come with me to enjoy a festive evening, one that includes paying homage to what Christmas is all about. Your choice." She started for the door.

"It's no choice at all," he grumbled.

"What did you say?" she asked over her shoulder.

"Nothing. Just getting my jacket." No wonder the kids obeyed her every command. Nicole had a way about her that cut through the baggage, giving a person nowhere to hide.

Maybe that was why he felt comfortable around her. She accepted him, that needy, scrawny kid and all. How would she react if he told her about Afghanistan? That he'd been powerless to save Seth and could only watch him die? Probably not as accepting.

Chapter 13

Nicole turned onto a quiet street in Union City. Halfway down the block, she pulled to the curb, braked, and slid the gearshift into park. "This is it. The house where I grew up."

Cam nodded and glanced around. The lots were small, a given considering land in Northern California was at a premium. The postage-stamp-sized yard was well maintained, the same as a few others in the vicinity.

Christmas lights filled the bushes and trees, and deflated blowup snowmen or reindeer were in the center of a few lawns. Bikes lay forgotten on the sidewalk across the street, and bent-up metal garbage cans lined the one-car garage. Next door someone had a car up on blocks in the driveway.

Cam immediately felt at ease. It was definitely a working-class neighborhood.

Colleen must have been watching from the window because the front door opened and she hurried out. "I'm so glad you decided to come." She sidled between the two and put an arm through each of their arms, leading them up the walk.

Inside, a giant Christmas tree, fully decorated, cramped the living room and blocked the only window.

Murphys appeared as fast as ants exiting their nest when disturbed. Cam counted nine, including Nicole and her mom. As the two stragglers, Nicole's oldest brother and her father, entered the room, he wondered how they'd all managed to grow up in such a small house. Obviously, size didn't matter. Love did.

The energy in the room went a long way toward making Cam feel even more at ease. Everything about this house and this family shouted welcome.

"We waited dinner on you, squirt." Kevin pulled on Nicole's

ponytail. "So are you going to introduce your friend?"

"Yes, give me a chance." Nicole took a deep breath and began. "This is Roberto Camareno. I get to call him Cam, since I'm a friend." She looked at Cam, and her head indicated the others one by one. "Cam, meet my brother Kevin." As they shook hands, she went on. "You already know Mary Ann and Kyle."

Mary Ann waved and Kyle nodded.

Nicole's hand gesture indicated three others. "Joseph is next to Kyle, then Maddie, and Caryn." She cleared her throat and added, "Across from them are Amanda, Thom Junior, and Charlie." They all acknowledged Cam with a wave or a tilt of the head. Nicole wrapped an arm around her father. "And this is Thom Senior."

Thom stuck out his hand. When they shook, Cam noted a firm grip.

"Now that we have that out of the way, would either of you like a drink?" Her dad released his hold on Cam's hand.

Nicole leaned over to whisper, "Mom makes a mean Christmas punch."

"Beware, though," Thom said. "Some claim it causes hair to grow on your chest."

"Hmm." Cam grinned. "Interesting." He glanced at Nicole and said in a low voice so that only she could hear, "How much alcohol is in one of those things?"

"Lots." Then as if realizing his intent, she shook her head. "But you don't have to drink anything."

"No, thanks," he murmured, shaking his head as one of Nicole's sisters handed him a drink. He'd forgotten her name already, so he just nodded. "I'm on call." That was his standard answer to avoid having to make lengthy explanations.

"No problem. I'll just get you a glass of plain punch."

Cam smiled. "That'd be nice."

Somehow they all found a place to sit. Cam felt like the guest of honor, as he got the one plush chair in the room. Three sat on the sofa, a couple dropped to the floor, and the others brought in chairs from the dining room.

"How about those Forty-Niners."

"They're a bunch of pansies. Couldn't even make it to the playoffs last year. My money's on the Steelers."

"You're a traitor."

Cam leaned back and listened to the comments coming fast and furious. There was no way he was joining in. Not with this crowd.

"Did you see what Kate was wearing? How can anyone look so good all the time? I wouldn't mind getting pregnant if I could look like she did when she was nine months along."

"You would look great too if you were British royalty."

"You're thinking of getting pregnant?" Cam recognized Colleen's voice.

"Yeah, she's got the staff and the money to buy the clothes. That's why she dresses so fabulously."

"So did Camilla, yet she always looked dowdy at the same age."

"Genes." Colleen turned to Mary Ann. "You never answered my question."

"Now you've done it," Kyle whispered to his wife.

"Is it so bad to want grandbabies?" Without waiting for a reply, Colleen waved a hand. "You're all a disappointment to me." It was hard to take her seriously considering the smile she sported while voicing the sentiment.

"You'll just have to be disappointed a while longer, Mom," Mary Ann chimed in. "Kyle and I aren't thinking about kids just yet."

"Don't wait too long or those eggs will dry up."

Mary Ann stuck her tongue out at the brother who spoke. "Funny."

Kevin, that was his name. With so many conversations going on at once, Cam had a hard time following them, or knowing who was speaking, for that matter. Boisterous was too tame a word. The Murphys were like a whirlwind, and Colleen was the force of the gale as the storm continued.

"Beyoncé left JayZ."

"I heard. That's such a tragedy."

"Kentucky has a good basketball team this year."

"I wonder if they'll beat UConn."

Thom, seated at the opposite end of the room from his wife, was more like the eye of the storm. Calm and watchful. "Who the hell is Beyoncé and JayZ?"

"Daddy, I can't believe you're so clueless."

"I wouldn't be clueless if someone would just tell me."

"She's a goddess who sings like an angel."

"Her moves aren't so angelic."

"They're bodilicious." The sister who spoke, Cam forgot her name already, stood and started doing an imitation of the singer.

"Save it for later," Colleen warned.

"I thought she was doing a fine imitation." Kevin paused. "Of JayZ."

Thom threw up his hands amid a burst of laughter. "I give up. Suddenly I don't want to know."

Cam laughed along with them. To say they all talked at once was an understatement. It was hard for anyone to get a word in edgewise unless they just chimed in. He didn't mind because he didn't have to participate. Just observe. And enjoy.

When Colleen announced that dinner was served, they crowded around the table filled with food. There was barely enough room for the plates and place settings.

Thom passed around the ham, cut in spiral curves. The others started on the side dishes in front of them, then passed them on.

"Pass more ham, please."

"Mom, these sweet potatoes are delicious. Did you do something different?"

"No. Same old recipe."

As Cam ate, the Murphys kept the conversation going. They cracked jokes about everyone and everything, including him. If he'd worried about being an odd man out, his worry had been for naught.

• • •

Around eleven fifteen, everyone piled into two cars for the trek to the church. Cam and Nicole sat in the backseat of the minivan. Thom drove, and Colleen navigated beside him.

Inside the vast church decorated with greenery complete with red and ivory bows, the Murphy clan genuflected, then slid single file into an empty pew quietly and respectfully—the complete opposite of their earlier rowdiness.

The organ blasted away and the choir sang "Oh Come All Ye Faithful." The tune brought back memories from his youth, before Cam's dad died and things were easier. His mom and dad sitting close, him nestled to her side. The smells and sounds of church assailed him.

Joyful and triumphant. The last time he'd sung those words was a year ago, minutes before the blast that changed his life so drastically. Even after death, life went on. Joy had to be found in the living and in the future. Did he dare believe in a future? The thought was definitely something to chew on.

As voices and music rang out, Cam felt the joy the Murphys had for celebrating together. That alone was a gift he'd cherish for a long time. Plus, they included him in the joy, which made it doubly so. For the next ninety minutes, peace settled over his being.

Looking around the room, he decided this was what Christmas was really about. Being with people and sharing.

He slanted a glance at Nicole and she winked. His smile broadened. How had she known this was exactly what he'd needed? The woman was an enigma. As the service ended and the priest told the congregation to go in peace, Cam caught Nicole watching him.

Her expression was so open and honest. Right then and there, he fell in love. Hard. Not the tumbling, easy roll of a gymnast, but the thudding clunk of a boulder hitting the ground in a landslide. Somehow he'd have to figure out a way to become someone worthy of her love.

He wasn't even sure that was possible, considering his sins as a rowdy teenager. He'd loved his mother too. Yet how had he shown that love? By getting drunk and cursing her, then going out and bashing in a few car windows. She'd had to work doubly hard to pay for his counseling. That was where he'd learned about anger and its debilitating force.

As Cam gave one last look around the church, a feeling like none other he'd experienced before surged forth, filling his soul with hope.

Nicole's voice drew him out of his thoughts.

"So, what'd you think?" She stuck her arm through his as they walked down the aisle. "Was I right?" Her smug expression said more than words ever could.

She clearly didn't need him to substantiate the question, so he didn't. "What now?"

"Marshmallows and hot chocolate while we sing Christmas carols."

"You're kidding?" He prayed it was so. Being around so much energy was draining.

"No. But I can see you've had enough of the Murphys for one night. Overdose too soon and you'll get an aversion to them."

"Can't have that." Though jesting, he was secretly relieved to spend the rest of Christmas day quietly. Preferably with her.

"No, we can't." Her expression morphed from playful to dead serious in a heartbeat. "I want you to stick around for a long, long time."

Cam bent to kiss her on the nose. "Don't worry. I'm not going anywhere." He captured her mouth, but before they became a spectacle, he broke the connection and grinned. "It'll take more than a few Murphys to keep me away."

Chapter 14

Thom Murphy clicked the garage door opener, then peered at Nicole in the rearview mirror. "Coming in for hot chocolate, Nikkie?"

She squeezed Cam's hand. "No, Dad. We're heading out. But thanks for asking." She grinned as he squeezed back. It had been fun to play like teenagers and hold hands all the way home from the church.

"We really appreciated you helping us bring in Christmas," Colleen said after Cam had hopped out. She gave him a quick hug. "Don't be a stranger."

A chorus of good-byes disturbed the early morning silence.

Colleen looked over her shoulder at her brood now filing into the house, then back at him. "You've obviously passed muster, so you're welcome anytime."

Nicole kissed her dad on the cheek. "Merry Christmas." Thom wrapped her in a bear hug. "I love you," he whispered.

She smiled. "I love you too." She gave her mom a quick hug and a kiss and said, "'Bye Mom."

"'Bye, dear." Colleen waved and turned toward the house. "You two be good," she said as she walked up the path. "And if you can't be good, play it safe and use a condom."

Cam nearly choked as he caught Nicole's gaze. "Did she just say what I thought she said?"

She cuffed him on the shoulder. "She's joking."

"That didn't sound like a joke to me." Cam followed her.

"Trust me, it is," she said. If only the ground would swallow her up about now. "Every time we'd go on a date in high school, she'd warn us about safe sex—called it reverse psychology." It had worked back then. But this time her mother's warped sense of humor wasn't funny. No, it pointed out that the last time she'd made a similar remark was when Seth was alive.

As Nicole clicked the keyless entry to unlock the car, he said, "I do have condoms, you know."

Ignoring the comment, Nicole climbed inside and waited for Cam to do the same.

"Is something wrong?" he asked when she'd driven a mile without speaking.

"I don't know if I can do this."

"Do what?"

His question, asked so innocently, had her blinking back tears that threatened. Unable to see clearly enough to drive, she pulled over to the side of the road and shifted into neutral. "Us."

Staring straight ahead, she wiped at her eyes and tried to sniff in a breath without giving away more of her emotional state. Everything had been so wonderful up until her mom had to go and spoil it. Obviously, Colleen had misinterpreted Cam's presence if she was able to joke about it. Joke or not, it hit home that no matter how far Nicole had come, she still wasn't over Seth's death.

Cam tucked a few stray hairs behind her ear. His touch was tender and made her feel even more fragile, if that were possible.

She risked glancing at him. "I can't make love with you. It's too soon." Disappointing her parents was one thing, but she hated the thought of disappointing Cam.

"Shush." He leaned toward her and kissed the side of her cheek. "No one's asking you to."

A tear leaked out and ran down the side of her face. Using his thumb, Cam wiped it away. Then he wrapped his hand around her neck and gently tugged her head closer. Their foreheads touched.

"I can wait," he whispered, rubbing his thumb over her cheekbone as if to smooth away her pain. His earnest gaze added to the moment.

It did help in a weird way. Just being free to express her feelings honestly eased ninety percent of the heartache.

"He died a year ago today," she said softly. "I almost forgot.

What kind of person does that make me?"

"A human one." He leaned back, his intent gaze focused on her. "And I'd venture to say Seth would want you to be happy."

"That's what my mom says." The rest of her pent-up tension dissipated in her long sigh.

"She's right. If I loved a woman and I died, the mere fact that I loved her would mean that I'd want her happiness over my own." His brow furrowed. "Isn't that what love is?"

She nodded.

When she offered a semblance of a smile, he kissed her brow. "Everyone deserves to be happy, you most of all." He released his hold on her.

Feeling as if the weight of the world had fallen off her shoulders, Nicole reached for the gearshift. As she drove the rest of the way to her apartment, her thoughts strayed to the sentiments Cam had just imparted. Coming from him, they sounded reasonable and sound. The fact that it was exactly one year to the day of Seth's death didn't go unnoticed. Nor could she discount one reality. The only other man besides Seth she'd ever been interested in beyond a passing fancy was sitting next to her, telling her he could wait.

Oh heavens. Those were Seth's exact words more than ten years ago when all her friends were into experimenting with sex and she wasn't ready. That was when she realized he truly loved her.

Sneaking a quick peek at Cam, she wondered if he might very well feel the same. Did she dare take the final step to giving herself to him? She already suspected she loved him. Yet the idea of making love terrified her. But it also filled her with hope.

Nicole pulled into the spot reserved for her.

"Why are we stopping here?" Cam shot her a direct look.

"This is where I live. I thought we could spend the night at my place. I have a Christmas tree and you don't," she added when his expression seemed to require a better explanation.

He nodded. "I can sleep on the couch, as long as it's not too lumpy." His eyes lit with humor. "You do have an extra toothbrush, I take it?"

"Don't worry. I gotcha covered."

They climbed out together. When she met him at the sidewalk, he slung his arm over her shoulder. "Lead on, fair maiden."

And she did, but along the way, she gave a quick glance at the heavens, along with a silent prayer to Seth. *I miss you, but I need to move on.*

• • •

"Are you sure you don't mind spending New Year's Eve with the senior crowd?" Cam asked, using the term his mother dubbed her friends at Windsor Manor. Dressed in a suit and tie, he trailed after Nicole, who was in the process of putting on makeup.

In the course of the last week, they'd fallen into a routine that worked for Cam. She brought enough stuff over to his apartment in order to be comfortable, and he did likewise at hers.

Despite not making love, they'd been inseparable during their off hours. It was winter break. Cam's new semester didn't begin for another three weeks. He'd cut back his hours at the rehab center. Most of the guys went home during Christmas and New Year's, so there wasn't a lot to be done.

Things were going well as far as Cam could tell. Nicole seemed happy. Even Seth, if he were still alive, couldn't find fault with their growing relationship. Cam was dying to make love to Nicole, but it wasn't just for sex. Being around her night and day was pure torture when the urge to show his feelings toward her also grew. Keeping his hands to himself wasn't easy, but he was after the whole enchilada, not some cheap thrills. He loved her enough to want the timing to be right. The thought should scare him, but it didn't. What terrified him was not measuring up to a man like Seth.

Finally, Nicole was ready. "How do I look?" She twirled, and the sheer red fabric followed her curvaceous body.

"Definitely worth the wait," he said, leaning in for a quick kiss. Then he grabbed her hand and headed for the door. If he didn't leave now, his good intentions could fly out the window. Hell, he was only human. "Come on, or we'll be late."

She laughed. "Wouldn't want that."

The drive to Windsor Manor took only minutes.

Now, as they stood outside his mother's unit, Nicole gasped when his mom opened the door in response to Cam's knock. "Conchetta, you look beautiful."

Cam nodded, doing his own double-take. "Yeah, Mom. You look stunning."

Conchetta put a hand to her face. Her blush added to the makeup's effect. Cam couldn't believe she was actually wearing mascara. It brought out her eyes. She appeared youthful and . . . happy.

Anthony stepped into view. A flash of annoyance flitted over Cam. He had mixed feelings about the guy's presence, but considering the change in his mother, it was hard not to be grateful. Cam was especially moved by the attention Anthony paid his mom as the group made their way to the dining room. The older man had the patience of a saint. Conchetta used his strong arm as an aid in order to walk a bit faster without relying on her cane. His mom always hated to be a burden to anyone, especially to him. Having someone else help her besides her son was a definite plus to Cam's way of thinking.

Conchetta stepped into the dining room, and an expression of awe crossed her face. "Oh my. It's absolutely beautiful."

The huge space was decorated like some fancy hotel ballroom. Two bottles of wine, one red and one white, rested on each table along with noisemakers and party hats. Streamers hung from the ceiling.

As Cam helped Nicole sit, he murmured close to her ear, so only she could hear, "Looks like these seniors know how to throw a party."

Nicole tossed out a half chuckle. "And the college girls are eating their hearts out because I'm with you instead of them."

Was that a hint of jealousy in her voice? Cam drew back to eye her intently, then breathed out a sigh of relief when nothing in her demeanor gave the thought any weight. "You've been here enough times for them to have figured out that we're an item," he said, just in case his assessment was wrong.

"Are we?" Nicole asked in a teasing tone.

"Are we what?" Cam reached for his napkin, then glanced at her when she hadn't responded after a few seconds. Her concerned expression stopped him cold.

"An item."

He cleared his throat and nodded. "Yeah. At least, that's my take on this past week. Do you have a different one?"

Her smile eased the tiny knot in his stomach that had formed within the last nanosecond, and the warmth in her gaze zinged heat all the way to his gut. He wrapped an arm around her and squeezed. "I'm a lucky man to have you all to myself on New Year's Eve." Her lips begged to be kissed. Without thinking, he leaned in and gave in to their demand.

One of the servers, a college girl, interrupted the moment to place a salad in front of him.

He broke away, let go of Nicole's shoulder, and sat up straight. "Thanks, Jasmine," he said in a matter-of-fact tone to stave off his embarrassment and Nicole's. Thankfully, the staff all wore nametags that had made it easier to learn their names over the last six months.

Jasmine nodded. "No thanks needed. Just doing my job. In fact, I should be the one thanking you two." She set Nicole's salad in front of her.

Cam glanced at the waitress. "How so?"

She grinned. "I won the bet."

"Bet? What bet."

"On whether or not you'd bring your lady friend tonight."

His jaw dropped open, and he and Nicole shared a quick glance. When she only shrugged, his attention returned to Jasmine. "You're kidding."

"No." The waitress spun around to grab two more salads from the carry tray behind her. After giving one to his mom and one to Anthony, she turned back to him. "Denny and Mike were positive you'd come solo, but I knew differently."

"Really?" Cam and Nicole said in unison.

Nodding, she placed her hands on her hips. "You two have the L-word written all over you."

Appearing nonchalant, he sneaked a peek at Nicole, who was paying an inordinate amount of attention to her salad. His focus moved to his mom.

Conchetta's smile was so wide, it practically touched both ears. "That makes me happy."

Anthony clapped him on the back and said, "Don't fight it."

Were his feelings that evident? Cam slanted Nicole a second glance. When all she did was smile and offer another shrug, his concern faded. Their growing relationship wasn't any big secret.

"Are you going to watch the Rose Bowl Parade tomorrow?" Cam threw the comment out in an effort to turn the conversation away from his and Nicole's relationship. Why get his mom's hopes up when he wasn't sure where things were going, or even if there was a destination, for that matter. Thankfully, his tactic worked.

Talk at the table eventually turned to the New Year's Eve festivities at Windsor Manor later that night. The facility had hired a live band to play from nine until twelve thirty in the reception area for anyone brave and energetic enough to dance.

As the wait staff began clearing the main course dishes to make room for dessert, Cam reached for Nicole's hand under the table and squeezed. He was glad she'd insisted they come here tonight instead of spending it with her family as she usually did.

The evening was turning out to be one of the best New Year's Eves ever, made more wonderful because his mom was clearly enjoying herself too. His mother's animated expression eased his worry over her happiness. As much as he wanted to claim responsibility, he knew it wasn't the case. Her joy was another result of Anthony's influence.

When the strawberries in whipped cream had been served, Jasmine brought out four champagne glasses. Melanie, the only waitress who wasn't a coed, trailed behind her with a bottle of Dom Pérignon, then proceeded to pour champagne into each one before handing them out.

Damn. Cam sat straighter. That was some pricey bubbly. His gaze cut to his mother, who had a hard time suppressing her excitement. What the hell was going on?

Anthony held up his glass, also looking mighty pleased with himself. "I'd like to propose a toast."

Obviously, he'd bought the champagne.

"To Conchetta." Anthony's gaze cut to Cam's mom, who beamed like a spotlight on a moonless night. "And to our life together, now that we have decided to take our relationship to the next level."

Deciding to go along, Cam clinked glasses with the others, yet trepidation crawled up his spine. Casually, he set his glass down and addressed his mom, keeping his voice neutral. "Next level?" What the hell did that mean?

"Yes," Conchetta said, looking directly at him, still all smiles. "I'm moving in with Anthony."

Cam almost choked and would have if he'd taken a sip of champagne just then. He took in a deep breath to gain control of his wits. His mother was an adult. Cam had to keep reminding himself of that fact in those few seconds. Yet the struggle to maintain a blank expression cost him his equilibrium. "I see," he finally said, smiling through gritted teeth because he damned well didn't see.

"It should work out perfectly. Anthony wants me to move in right away so that we can be together all the time." Her expression became almost shy as she gazed at the man with adoration. He, in turn, patted her hand.

Shaking his head, Cam narrowed his gaze to look first at his mom and then at Anthony before going back to his mother. "Isn't this rather sudden?"

"The lease on my apartment is up on February first, and that gives us plenty of time for a thirty-day notice." Her smile brightened, if that were at all possible. "That way you don't have to spend your money taking care of me."

Absorbing her bombshell, Cam just stared at her before finally finding his voice. "What about marriage?"

"We don't need that at our age," Anthony chimed in, followed by Conchetta's firm nod.

Cam wiped his face, using the motion as a stall while trying to think of something positive to say. When nothing came to mind, he blurted, "Mom, this is crazy."

"No, it's not. It's a blessing. We love each other and just want to be together. Is that so wrong?"

"Without marriage?" Had some other person taken over his mother's body? She was a devout Catholic. That was why she'd stayed married to his deadbeat dad until his tragic death left them even more penniless.

About to take a drink, his mom set her glass on the table and leaned toward him. "This is the twenty-first century, you know. People do it all the time."

"Of course I know that." Two of his coworkers had live-in situations with their significant others. And if he really thought about it, he and Nicole were technically living together.

But that's different, and it's not your mother.

Still speechless from shock, Cam took a minute to respond. "What happens if something goes wrong?"

"It won't." His mother crossed her arms and didn't blink an eye, just continued meeting his gaze. Her resolute expression was too much to swallow. He looked to Nicole for help. "You talk some sense into her."

Shoving his chair away from the table, he stood. As he turned to make his way out of the room, Conchetta rose.

"No." Anthony placed a hand on her arm. "I think I should go, since I'm the one who's stealing his mother away."

Chapter 15

Nicole stood, about to chase after Cam, but Conchetta stopped her. "I know my *niño* is upset, but he and Anthony have to work this out between them, *sí?*"

Though not entirely sure it was the right thing to do, she sat back down. "You have to admit, your news is a bit shocking."

The older woman smiled, her eyes alit with a spark of humor. "Yes, I'm sure he sees it that way. Roberto means well. If asked, I would gladly tell him how it is between Anthony and myself. Anthony is lonely, and I . . . Well, let's just say he has convinced me that we're a good match." She picked up her flute and took a hefty drink of champagne. "I'm old, but not old enough to be in this facility. When caring and companionship come knocking, I'm not willing to turn my back on either."

Nodding, Nicole stared at the door Cam and Anthony had just exited, debating whether she should go and check on things. Just in case.

Oblivious to her concern, Conchetta fingered the stem of her glass. "My first marriage wasn't happy. For anyone." She patted Nicole's hand. "Alcoholism is a horrible disease, and when mental pain is a contributing factor, it's almost impossible to overcome." Conchetta paused, sadness taking over her expression that only moments ago was all smiles and happiness. "My husband witnessed drug dealers viciously kill his family when he was barely nineteen. From that point on, he hadn't been able to function without dulling the horrendous memories with something."

Understanding about Cam's issues finally dawned on Nicole as Conchetta continued speaking.

"We married right before we escaped to this country, but I

still had my mama and papa, and aunts and cousins. He had no one. I don't think he ever got over the fact that he survived by hiding in a closet, helpless to do anything to stop the carnage. I know he felt guilty about that." She glanced up and a wistful smile appeared. "It's just too bad my husband's demons took over his soul before our son was born."

Her smile widened a bit. "My Cam inherited a strong sense of responsibility from his papa." She shook her head, exhaling a long sigh. "Yet all Cam knew of him was the drinking, the remorse, and the continued promises to change. For a while my husband would be the caring and lovable man I married, until the relapse when his pain become too much to bear."

"How sad," Nicole murmured, for want of anything else to say.

"It was not a happy time. His death was a blessing, freeing him from the hell he spent on earth. That's how it is for some, you know. And for those of us left behind, we have to find happiness any way we can."

"I'm glad you told me all of this. It must've been hard on Cam. And you."

"Yes, it was for both of us, and life goes on. My son was my future. I knew he could go far if given the tools, yet I was limited by my lack of education and skills. So I cleaned houses." Conchetta held up her misshapen hand. "Cam blames himself for my arthritis. There is no blame to lay on anyone. It is life. We live it to the fullest by making the best of what the good Lord gives us."

Nicole thought about Seth and her year spent grieving. It *was* the living who suffered. The dead, gone from this earth, no longer felt pain or sorrow.

"Will you talk to my *niño*? Make sure he understands he need not worry about me. I know my decision to move in with Anthony is rather sudden, but we have a solid connection that few are lucky to share. I'm grasping what little pleasure I have found in the life I have left."

"Of course I will." Nicole moved to stand in front of Conchetta's chair. "Thanks for confiding in me. I'll talk to him."

109

As she bent to give the woman a gentle hug, one thought filled her with hope. Finally free from the grieving bonds of Seth's death, she'd be foolish not to take advantage of what God put in her path—namely Roberto Camareno and the connection they'd made.

• • •

Outside, Cam paced. How could his mother even consider making such a drastic move without talking to him first to get his advice ... or help? The guy could be someone who preys on lonely women.

The door opened and he froze, despite expecting the one person he didn't want to see heading his way.

"I know you're upset." Anthony halted a few feet away from him. "But try to see it from Conchetta's point of view. She's a grown woman who's had to depend on her son for much too long. It's time to let her go."

Cam stepped into the guy's space and glowered at him. "So you can hurt her?" The comment was meant to be belligerent, but he realized it also vented the most valid of his concerns.

Anthony met his stare with a calm reserve that unnerved him. Thankfully, Anthony finally looked away. He ran a hand through his thick silver hair and sighed. "I have no intentions of hurting her." That composed stare was back. "We've found we have a lot in common and enjoy each other's company. Conchetta makes me laugh. I feel like a teenager when I'm with her, and that is something a seventy-year-old man like me treasures. I learned when I buried my wife that life is too short for regrets."

Clenching his fist, Cam stilled the urge to plow into the guy. Instead of hitting him, he said, "Then why not offer marriage?"

"My reasons are monetary in nature." When Cam raised his eyebrows and waited for him to continue, he said, "My children, all grown adults, must come first and foremost. If I marry Conchetta and I die before her, she'll inherit half of the small fortune I've spent my life building. I cannot dishonor my children or their mother by allowing that to happen when my dearly departed wife sacrificed much and worked alongside me to make it possible." He paused and met Cam's gaze directly. "Conchetta is well aware of my position, and I've agreed to provide for her in my will."

"So in a nutshell, it all boils down to greed." From the beginning there was always something he didn't like about the guy, and now he fully understood what that was.

"Please try to understand." Anthony held up a hand. "I will treat her as a wife. We're right for each other, and I don't plan on having any regrets when it comes to your mother."

"I'll bet." Cam's lip curled upward.

"Why can't you see that she's happy and be happy for her?"

Unable to refute Anthony's latest claim, he leaned closer and practically snarled, "You'd better make sure you keep her happy, or you'll have me to contend with." After speaking his piece, he walked back inside the dining room, appearing much calmer than he felt.

When he reached Nicole, he nodded. "We're leaving."

Nicole's brow furrowed. "But it's barely after ten. On New Year's Eve."

"I don't want to talk about it." He went to retrieve her wrap before either Nicole or his mother said anything else to delay him. The mood he was in, he was ready to hit someone. Preferably Anthony. That would only cause a scene.

Upon returning, he noticed Anthony had come back to the table. The older man remained silent as Cam helped Nicole out of her chair.

He glanced at his mother. Big mistake.

Conchetta's gaze was beseeching. "Please, *niño*, try to understand."

Cam looked away before her expression could sway him. "I love you, Mom. But I'm too upset to speak right now. I might end up saying something I'll regret." He leaned in and kissed her cheek. "I'll call you in a few days to see if you need anything."

With that, he grabbed Nicole's hand and practically dragged her out of the facility.

Chapter 16

"Do you want to talk about it?"

Nicole's worried voice drew Cam out of his deep thoughts.

After leaving Windsor Manor, they had ended up back at Cam's apartment—after he'd tried to use his *I prefer to be alone* spiel. Unfortunately, she hadn't bought it. Hence, now they were lying in his king-sized bed with her most likely about to ask more prying questions.

Just thinking about the bombshell his mother had dropped earlier set his heart pounding out of control. Exactly as it had when Nicole had broached the subject on the car ride here. Then, to make matters worse, other insecurities came out. If he couldn't take care of his mother, how in the hell could he take care of Nicole? Despite the debilitating frustration that overwhelmed him, the need in his gut to curl into Nicole and forget everything overshadowed even that.

"I don't want to think about my mother, I don't want you to think about Seth. I just want to think about *us*." He lowered his head. "And *this*." His mouth ravaged hers. When he realized he was using the kiss to expel the demons in his heart, he rolled over and lay on his back with his hand over his face. Hell, he was letting emotion get the better of him just as it had all those years ago, right after his dad's death. "I'm sorry." Rubbing his eyes with a thumb and forefinger, he let out an audible sigh. "You didn't deserve that."

"No." She placed her hand on his midsection. Then, lifting his T-shirt, she leaned in and trailed a few kisses over his exposed belly. "I didn't."

Her lips were warm and soothing. In response, he slid his hand up and down her arm. She had the softest skin, and her touch was healing. Cam didn't know what he'd do if she weren't here now. Yet she deserved so much more than he could give her. Eventually, he'd have to let her go. How in the hell was he going to find the strength to do so?

He swallowed hard. "I'm pretty upset." He opened one eye to peer at her through his fingers. "Guess you figured that out, huh?"

She nodded. "I had a clue when we left a New Year's Eve party before the dancing began."

He groaned. "And even the senior crowd is still partying hearty." His gaze lowered. "I'm sorry I lost it. My mom is really important to me and . . ." Christ, he didn't know how he felt. His insides were tied in a giant knot.

Nicole placed a hand on his arm and squeezed. "You could be happy for her." Her hand moved to his chin, and using a thumb and forefinger, she forced him to look at her. "She's found someone to love."

"Someone who could very well hurt her."

"Love always involves a risk. From my perspective, it appears as if she's willing to take the risk." When Cam remained silent, she added, "She still needs you, but as a son, not a provider."

"What happens if I can't be what she needs?" That thought scared him shitless. It had been easy to pay her bills and make sure she was doing well. Without doing all that, how did he show her he cared? He certainly hadn't done a very good job of being a worthy son during his teens. If he had, she wouldn't be suffering such crippling arthritis now.

"Oh, Cam. Most mothers would die for a son like you."

"Most sons would die for a mother like her," he whispered. "She worked so hard all those years making sure I had what I needed." Just thinking about all she'd sacrificed to ensure his success made his throat grow tight. "She suffered greatly my last three years of high school. Cleaning houses when she could barely move. I'm ashamed I didn't do more for her then."

"Did you love her, like you do now?"

Incensed, he sat up. "What kind of question is that?" Cam sought her gaze and held it. "Hell yes, I loved her."

"Did you show her how you felt?"

He lay back down and let out a lengthy exhale in an effort to relax. "I'm not sure I know how to do that." Nicole's probing questions were only an attempt to help, not criticize. "But I tried."

It might have been easier if he hadn't started hanging with the wrong element in high school. Thankfully, his mother had realized their environment's role in his problem and became a full-time maid for a woman who also provided a guest house in a better school district. The only downside was the woman acted as if she owned his mother. That was also when Conchetta's physical problems began. All because Cam got into trouble.

"Then don't stop trying." Nicole kissed his neck. "Showing our love is all any of us can expect from one another."

Her words made a hell of a lot of sense and did much to ease the ache in his soul. "You're wise beyond your years. You know that?" If only he'd shown his mother more love and support back then, she might not be crippled with arthritis. She wasn't even sixty yet, but her joints were those of a ninety-year-old. The only way Cam knew how to make amends was by taking care of her. If Conchetta moved into Anthony's house . . .

"I have a good role model. My mom," Nicole said, breaking into his thoughts. "And she is very wise."

Cam trailed his hand up her arm, then back down in slow motion, and smiled. "Moms are like that."

"Your mom's also wise."

"Oh?"

"Um-hmm. We had a nice conversation. I think she knows what she wants and is willing to go after it. Enough about moms." She rolled over on top of him. "Where were we?"

He gripped her arms to push her off. "Wait—" Locking lips with her now wasn't a good idea.

Without heeding his protest, she nipped at his chin. "You were kissing me, that's where." She grazed his lips and his willpower took a major hit. "I should warn you," she murmured. "I'm willing to go after what I want too."

When her mouth lowered to connect with his, the remaining

resolve to keep her at arm's length had been totally knocked out of him. Loving her was definitely worth any risk, and thanks to her nearness, the craving coiled within his gut had already unwound past the point of no return.

Groaning and accepting the kiss, he deepened it. If he lived to be a hundred, he'd never get enough of kissing her. "Is this where we were?" he murmured breathlessly when she finally broke their connection.

Nodding, she leaned back and one-handedly lifted her T-shirt over her head to reveal a black lace bra that belonged in a Victoria's Secret catalog. "And then we were about to make love," she whispered, capturing his lips again.

He froze as her meaning registered. He sat up and turned to gaze into her eyes. "You're sure?" His erection was rock hard and bulging with need that had simmered for too long. Shoving the need back under control would be pure hell, but it would be a bigger hell to know she wasn't ready.

She grinned and reached for him, drawing his head close to hers. "I'm taking my own advice about risk." Their lips barely touched. He held his breath as she added, "I'm very ready."

Even as he knew he didn't deserve this, he surrendered to the craving and sank into her heat.

Recriminations would come later.

Then everything faded away until only Nicole was there. Loving him.

• • •

The next morning, Nicole woke up without the usual sensation of sadness that had permeated her life since Seth's death. She glanced at the man next to her, his unshaven face relaxed in slumber. Smiling, she restrained the urge to toss back the dark brown lock of hair that fell over his left eye, and hugged herself instead.

Nicole would always love Seth, her first love and someone she'd intended to spend her life with. For an entire year, the idea of loving anyone else was unfathomable. Yet last night she'd taken a huge step in another direction. Her heart definitely had the capacity to heal, even after being torn apart with grief. Right now it was near to bursting with love. In part, she had Conchetta's willingness to jump into her relationship with Anthony as an impetus for her decision to take a risk.

Gently lifting the covers so as not to wake Cam, she slipped out of bed and headed for the bathroom. Along the way, the memory of last night and Cam's reaction played in her mind's eye. He'd been so upset. She hoped he'd eventually come to understand that he wasn't losing a mother. He was gaining a father ... well, figuratively speaking, she thought, brushing her teeth. Cam obviously needed another dose of the Murphys' love. She rinsed her mouth, turned off the water, and headed toward the kitchen for a much-needed caffeine infusion.

Nicole had all the vices in their relationship, her caffeine addiction topping the list. Cam wasn't a coffee drinker, nor did he drink anything stronger than an occasional beer to her glass of wine each night with dinner. Yet the day after Christmas, Cam made sure his cupboard was stocked with both, a totally considerate thing to do on his part. That was Cam—thoughtful to the core.

Grinding fresh beans—the darker the better—took only seconds, as did setting up the machine with the proper amount of water. She hit the ON button, then grabbed her cell phone. While waiting for the coffee to brew, she called her mom.

"Hi, sweetie," Colleen said, coming onto the line a few rings later. "What's up?"

"I was wondering if I could bring Cam by for the usual Murphy New Year's breakfast." Nicole had had a whole week to prepare for the normal teasing that bringing home a "special friend" on New Year's Day would inspire.

"Sure. But—" Colleen broke off. "It's still pretty early. The others won't be up for another hour or so."

"That's okay."

"What's okay," Cam asked, coming up behind her and kissing her neck. She stepped around him and gave him a stern look while covering up the phone. "Shush. I'm talking to my mom."

"Is that Cam?" Her delight came through loud and clear in a

quick laugh.

Tossing her hair behind one ear and turning away from Cam, Nicole cleared her throat. "Yes." She slapped at his hands as he tried to pull her into a bear hug.

"Tell him I said hi."

"Tell her hi back," Cam said, obviously hearing her mom's part of the conversation. He yanked open a cabinet door and removed a bowl, filled it with honey nut oats, and then retrieved the milk out of the fridge. Seconds later he was carrying his breakfast over to the table.

"Mom, I gotta go. We'll be there in an hour." She hung up. Casting the phone aside, she yelled, "Wait! Don't take another bite." She grabbed his bowl out from under him.

"I'm hungry."

When he stood to try to take it back, she shook her head and headed for the sink. "We're going to my mom and dad's house for breakfast." She placed the bowl in the sink and turned, almost bumping into him.

He didn't step away, just put his hands on the countertop, one on each side of her, effectively blocking her in. Then he leaned in to nuzzle her neck. "I thought we could have a nice quiet morning here."

"We can do that later, but the traditional New Year's Day breakfast is only celebrated at the Murphys' on the first day of the year."

His expression deepened into a scowl.

"Don't pout." Nicole patted his cheek. "You'll have a great time." When he took her hand and started kissing her palm, then her wrist, a heat spread up her arm and a warm sensation traveled all the way to her center. "Stop that," she said in her firmest tone of voice. "Seducing me won't work."

Cam's eyebrows shot up. "Are you saying you'd rather spend our first morning together after *last night* at your mom and dad's house?"

Her smiled died. *Shoot.* When he put it like that, it no longer seemed like such a great idea. Still, if she backed out now, the teasing would be worse because everyone would figure out why they weren't coming. "Hmm. Not really, but the die is cast." She ducked out from under his arms and turned toward the bedroom to finish dressing. "Besides, it won't take but a few hours, and then we'll have the rest of the day to be together."

"Who all is going to be there?" Cam said twenty minutes later as she eased her Mazda out of his apartment complex parking lot.

"Everyone, as far as I know."

"I don't know why I let you talk me into this," he murmured, glancing out the passenger window. "Your family can be intimidating in a group."

Accelerating onto the freeway, Nicole placed her hand on his arm resting on the console and gave a slight squeeze. "I know they can be a bit to swallow at times, but they mean well." She offered a wan smile when he caught her gaze. "It means a lot to me that you're coming along. I was a basket case last year and stayed in my room for the first couple of weeks after Seth died. This year, I want to celebrate. Besides," she said as she punched the gas pedal to merge into light traffic. "It'll do you good to be around my family. That way you'll appreciate yours more."

Cam only grunted and remained silent until she pulled onto her parents' street.

If Cam had been worried about her family's reaction to their relationship, it had definitely been for naught, Nicole thought as Colleen hugged them and held the door open wide. The enormous smile she offered was more than welcoming.

Thom, sporting a similar grin as his wife, wrapped Nicole in a bear hug. Then he shook Cam's hand and clapped him on the back. "Come in. We have mimosas all ready."

Nicole shot Cam a quick glance and groaned. She'd forgotten about the mimosas. "You don't have to have champagne in yours," she whispered.

"I know." The smile he bestowed on her sent funny signals to her tummy. "I'm beginning to realize not everyone is like my father."

Unsure of exactly what that meant, she nodded. Did he think they were all lushes just because her family liked to celebrate? Now was not the time to ask for clarification, though. The

Murphy clan would pick up on it, which could easily lead to a barrage of questions.

One by one, her brothers and sisters appeared, looking like death warmed over, thanks to the Murphy New Year's Eve bash. Nicole's mom and dad were famous for their parties, especially the last one of the year.

None of her siblings would dare miss it without a good excuse. At Thom's insistence that his kids not drive after so much celebrating, they ended up spending the night.

"How's the job search going?" Colleen handed Nicole a flute filled with orange juice and champagne.

"Great." Nicole had given Mary Ann notice at Unlimited Accessories. "I start back at Taylor Elementary in a week."

"That's wonderful, dear." Colleen then turned to Mary Ann, who'd stumbled out seconds earlier. "Maggie will be delighted to know you'll need us a little longer." She and Maggie had picked up Nicole's extra shifts while she'd spent the last few days preparing her résumé to send out to every school district within thirty miles—just in case.

Mary Ann nodded. Groaning, she waved away the mimosa her mother was trying to hand her. "I need coffee."

Her mom grinned. "You and Kyle certainly know how to dance." She glanced at Nicole. "They cut up the room. You missed a great party." Herding them toward the kitchen, following Mary Ann, she asked, "So, how was your party? Did you two have a nice time?"

"We had a great time," Cam interjected when Nicole looked at him, and the memory of last night passed between them. Her flaming face was a dead giveaway to what happened.

A warm, mushy sensation filled her. Praying her mother wasn't looking at her, she ducked her head to hide a smile. Thank heavens for Cam—in more ways than one. He, along with a little aid from his mom, was responsible for helping her fend off her grief and depression that had paralyzed her for all of last year.

In the kitchen, Colleen finished passing out mimosas, then held up her glass. "Here's to a loving and prosperous new year."

"I'll drink to that," Cam said, clinking glasses with the others present, his filled with just orange juice.

Colleen laughed. Then her assessing glance landed on Nicole. "It's good to have you back, sweetie."

Amid the teasing laughter, well-being flowed through Nicole's system. "It's good to be back," she said, understanding the full importance of the moment.

Scents of bacon and maple syrup wafted under Nicole's nose. Her stomach gurgled, and those close enough to hear it cracked a few more jokes about the noise.

"What do you expect? I'm hungry." She tried to act affronted, but no one bought it, considering she couldn't stop grinning.

"Must've been a pretty exhausting night," Kevin murmured behind her.

If you only knew. Subduing a smile, Nicole simply nodded. "It was. We partied with the senior crowd, as Conchetta would say."

Colleen grabbed some plates from the cupboard. "Well, tell us about it."

"Dinner was fantastic." Nicole set about helping her mother carry platters of food to the sideboard in the dining room, the whole time talking about what they'd eaten the night before and the decorations. "The band played until well after midnight," she said, ending her spiel without letting on that they'd left early. What her family didn't know wouldn't hurt them.

Once all the food was spread out buffet-style, Nicole reached for a plate and loaded it up.

"Go ahead, Cam. It's first come, first served. There are too many mouths to feed in this house to stand on ceremony." Colleen picked up a plate and began piling sausage and pancakes on it. "Next year, you should bring Conchetta to our New Year's Eve party, and we'll show you both how the Murphys do it right."

"We'll have to get a bigger house," Thom said, giving his wife a brief squeeze on the shoulders. "It wasn't so crowded with nine kids along with the adults, but now that everyone is grown and bringing their significant others . . ." He sighed and broke off, glancing at the ceiling. "Maybe we can knock out some walls and make the living room into a great room?"

Colleen glanced at him with a bit of annoyance, a look that said his elevator clearly didn't go all the way to the top floor. "Then where will the grandkids sleep?"

Thom only laughed. "What grandkids? The way your children are stalling, you may never have any."

"Dad, you're usually on our side," Caryn, Nicole's oldest sister said, pouring herself a mimosa.

"Yes, well, I'm starting to see your mother's point."

"Oh God, here it comes. Wait for it . . ." Kevin rolled his eyes. "Now you've done it. It's too early, and my head hurts too much to listen to complaints about shirking our child-producing duty."

"Yeah, Dad. We *do* have plenty of time." Caryn picked up a piece of bacon and began munching, adding in between bites, "Especially in this day and age."

"Maybe so," Colleen said. "But all those actresses and celebrities who are having babies well into their forties are lucky to have tens of thousands of dollars to spend on fertility clinics and youth-defying products." She waved her fork to indicate the others around the table. "You all aren't that lucky, and if you don't hurry up, your window of opportunity will shrink."

"Among other things," Kevin said.

"At least she's off the eggs-dying kick."

Colleen looked at Cam. "You're our only hope."

"Excuse me?" Cam cut Nicole a quick glance before his focus returned to her mom. "I don't follow."

"Obviously you and Nicole have hit it off. Now that Nicole's back to teaching kindergarten, I'd venture to say she's back to wanting half a dozen kids too." She cut off a piece of sausage and gave Nicole a pointed look. "You're pushing thirty. I started in my early twenties, and I could've used a few more years in between babies."

Nicole resisted the urge to crawl under the table. Heavens, her mom had them having six kids already. That was way worse than if she'd had them walking down the aisle. Nicole had to put a stop to her ranting. Talk of babies and weddings would easily scare any man off, Cam included.

"Mom, we've barely started seeing each other. It's only been a couple of weeks." A person so bent on having grandkids should have more tact and patience.

Nicole flashed Cam an *I'm sorry* glance, then in an effort to get the talk to anything but their relationship, she said, "Cam's mother is moving in with Anthony Morales, the man she met at the gala."

"Really?" Mary Ann glanced up. "That was only a couple of weeks ago."

Nicole stuck a bite of pancakes into her mouth, realizing her error in mentioning Cam's mom, considering Colleen's triumphant expression as she said, "When it's right, it's right."

"I'm sure they've talked about it," Thom said, apparently missing the looks shooting back and forth between mother and daughter—or maybe because of it—Nicole wasn't sure. "When you get to be our age, relationships change. They're more about companionship and having someone special to head into old age with." Thom grasped his wife's hand and took it to his lips. "Isn't that right, sweetheart?" He gave a brief kiss and, keeping hold of her mom's hand, sent Nicole a secret wink.

Colleen's smile reached her eyes as she nodded. "Precisely. Life would be so hard without your father."

Nicole chanced a peek at Cam, and something passed between them. Unable to decipher exactly what it was, she picked up her mimosa and took a sip.

What would her future hold? She surely didn't know, but more than anything, she wanted Cam to be part of it.

Chapter 17

"So, what do you want to do tomorrow?" Nicole clicked away on her laptop, looking for deals. It had become a contest of sorts during the last few weeks to find the cheapest entertainment for their days off.

She spotted something interesting in the browser and connected to the site. "There's a free concert in Berkeley."

This was their last weekend together before Cam had to return to his full schedule, and she wanted to make this time memorable. Not that any moment spent with Cam wasn't memorable.

He shook his head. "Too far away."

"How about the Mystery House. I found a coupon that gets us in for half price, considering it's January and tourists are scarce this time of year."

Cam looked over her shoulder, read the screen, and then scrunched up his nose. "Sounds barbaric and weird. Her husband made all that money with rifles, and she tries to make amends by building all these rooms?" He motioned with his hand to keep going. "What else?"

Exasperated, she shut the laptop. "Let's take BART to the city and pretend we're tourists. We can have coffee at the Buena Vista and take a cable car ride."

"We did that last weekend." He pulled her onto his lap and nuzzled her neck. "How about a fancy dinner out on the town? Now that I'm not paying for my mother's care, I can afford to take you to a decent restaurant."

"But—"

He cut off what she was about to say about not spending money with a kiss. Turning for better access, she wrapped her arms around him as a tidal wave of emotion swamped her.

"Hmm," she said, moving her lips to his chin, then to his ear. "I have a better idea. Let's call out for takeout and stay here."

"A lady after my own heart," he whispered, recapturing her mouth.

His cell phone rang. Cam broke the kiss and reached for it, then checked the screen. "I need to take this." He made the connection and put the phone to his ear. "Hi, Mom."

Of course he had to take Conchetta's call. As far as Nicole knew, Cam hadn't seen her since New Year's Eve.

"What's up?" Cam spent a moment listening before nodding. "So you're really doing this, huh?" Another long pause followed; Conchetta was obviously talking. "Sure, I'd be glad to help. Let me see if Nicole is free and she can help too." He winked at her, then grinned. "Yeah, I'm sure the two of you will have a great time setting up your kitchen while Anthony and I handle the big stuff."

Cam hung up and nuzzled her neck. "Now, where were we?"

Nicole leaned her head away, giving him a curious look. "What was that all about?"

"My mom's moving in with Anthony tomorrow. She called to see if I could help." He wrapped a hand around her neck and pulled her toward him. "My day off just got booked," he murmured, his lips barely touching her mouth.

The almost-kisses sent a jolt of heat toward her middle. If she weren't flesh and blood, she'd probably melt from the intensity in his gaze. "And you're invited." He took another nibble on her lip. "Wanna help her move with me?"

"Sure," she was able to squeak out. It was tough to concentrate on what he was asking with those lips doing such decadent things to her neck as they roamed toward her ear and back to her mouth. The question concerning his mother that had resided on the tip of her tongue quickly faded into the far reaches of her mind as Cam's mouth covered hers.

Seconds later he stood, pulled her up, and stepped them toward his big bed without breaking contact. A moan escaped her when her calves hit the mattress and he gave a slight push. Both landed on the soft space. At this point, Cam knew all of her weaknesses, and it seemed he was using them in a siege to win her heart. An unnecessary act, since he already owned it.

He began unbuttoning her blouse in slow motion. Her breath hitched in the back of her throat in anticipation. After each button, he bent over and spent an exorbitant amount of time kissing the skin underneath. Second by second, minute by minute, he continued his ministrations until he got to her bra. In a deft move, he unsnapped it with one hand while the other released another button to expose even more of her chest. The air felt cool on her skin until the warmth of his mouth moved lower, adding to the heat building inside her belly. No one did lovemaking as slow and tender as Cam.

Impatient for what came next, Nicole reached for him, only to have her wrists caught in his hand as he lifted her arms over her head and held them there while that mouth of his drove her more crazy with desire. Unfortunately, there was definitely a disadvantage to slow and tender. Cam damn well took forever to undress her. It made for an explosive orgasm, all this foreplay. Anytime she'd try to hurry him along with a touch or a rub, he'd still her hands. The third time she struggled to pull out of his hold, he halted with a hand on her breast and peered into her eyes.

"Do you trust me?"

Oh heavens. Looking into that expressive gaze was as if he was giving her a glimpse of his soul. And it was absolutely beautiful.

"Yes." She trusted him enough to fall in love with him.

His hand continued stroking in all the right places. The sensations swirled inside her again—sensations so strong they stole most of her air. She said in between huffs of breath, "But I only wanted to give you some of the same pleasure you always give me."

Nicole had already surrendered her whole heart to Cam, but she held back from verbalizing her feelings.

Cam might feel the same way, but there were times when he'd shut her out. Until she was sure of his love, remaining silent was her best course of action.

• • •

"Rise and shine, Beauty."

Cam's teasing voice cut through her haze of sleep. Squinting, she put up a hand to block out the bathroom light hitting her face. It was still dark outside. "What time is it?" She turned over and pulled the covers around her shoulders.

"It's a little after six. Mom said we need to be there at six thirty, so get a move on."

She groaned, remembering their plans for the day. "It should be a crime to have to get up before dawn on Saturdays," she grumbled, grimacing as she climbed out of the bed.

"I do it all the time." When she tossed him a withering look, his smile broadened. "Don't be grumpy." He leaned in to kiss her on the cheek and handed her the to-go cup he'd hidden behind his back. "I made you some coffee."

"A man after my own heart." Nicole snatched the cup out of his hand, took a deep draft, and closed her eyes as she savored the rich flavor. "Thank God for coffee." She opened her eyes and glanced at Cam, who was grinning at her as if she were the most entertaining thing he'd ever seen. "How can you be so cheerful this early without caffeine?"

"Who needs stimulants when I have you?"

Rolling her eyes and heading for the bathroom, she mumbled, "It's still not natural."

Twenty minutes and another cup of coffee later, Nicole and Cam exited the elevator on Conchetta's floor after signing in at the front desk.

"Good thing we were early." Cam knocked on his mother's front door. "I thought they'd never quit with the 'we'll miss you and your mother' downstairs.'"

"This is a nice place," Nicole said, nodding. "Everyone seems so friendly."

"Yeah, it's why I never minded paying so much." He gave her a pointed look. "And why I worry about this move."

Anthony opened the door. "Right on time." He indicated Conchetta with the tilt of his head. "She's got it all organized, so the move should go smoothly." He stepped aside.

Nicole and Cam moved past him into the living room now filled with boxes.

"Wow, Mom, you really didn't need my help."

His mother grinned. "Maria, Anthony's daughter, spent a few days here helping me pack. She's a sweet girl."

Nicole and Cam shared a quick glance.

"Girl?" Cam's brow lifted.

Conchetta laughed. "Well, maybe not girl, since she's in her thirties." Using her cane, she hobbled to the bar separating the kitchen from the living room. "I found some pictures you might like while I was packing." She pointed to the counter.

Cam opened the shoe box.

Nicole moved to his side as Anthony said, "I wanted to hire movers, but Conchetta didn't want me to spend the money."

"That's my mom. Gotta love her thriftiness," Cam whispered to Nicole, closing the box and setting it aside.

Anthony chuckled, obviously overhearing. "My son should be here any minute with his truck."

As if on cue, a knock sounded. Anthony opened the door and made hasty introductions to his son Anthony Junior, who stepped into the room with a dolly behind him.

He gave a two-fingered wave. "Just call me Tony."

"We'll load the boxes first," Anthony said.

Dolly in tow, Tony moved to where his father pointed and commenced loading the boxes onto it. Once full, he pushed it toward the door, saying over his shoulder, "There's a loading elevator and exit in the back of the building. The truck is parked right outside the exit."

• • •

"See, it's not so bad," Nicole said to Cam an hour later. "I think their relationship will work out fine. They certainly get along well together, don't you agree?"

Cam nodded as Nicole punched the gas pedal to catch up to Tony's truck. "Yeah." As hard as it was to swallow, he couldn't dispute her claim. "We emptied the apartment in record time."

Anthony had given them his address, but Nicole hadn't

bothered to put it into the GPS. Since she was having no problem staying with the truck that followed behind Anthony's baby-blue Cadillac, Cam didn't feel the need to either.

"Tony seems like a nice guy," she said.

"Yeah. He is." Cam liked him right from the get-go.

"Nice enough to be the brother you never had?"

He sighed and looked out the passenger window. "I won't go that far, but . . ."

How would it be to have grown up with a man like Anthony as a father? Cam was starting to like him. More than a little. Obviously, he'd hastily judged the man before getting to know him.

The sun was up and shining brightly, promising a beautiful day. It might as well be gloomy and dreary, considering how low his mood had plummeted over the last two hours.

"Mom seems really happy." Too late, Cam was starting to realize his mother had just been going through the motions of life since his return from Afghanistan, just like him. Or maybe because of him. Why hadn't he understood more about her emotional needs and tried to meet them? It probably meant he was more like his father than he'd thought.

Surreptitiously, he watched Nicole as she nimbly maneuvered the car through the narrow streets. They were getting in too deep, and he sensed he wasn't what she needed either. He loved her enough to want her to be happy. Deep down inside, he knew he wasn't the person to make her happy, when he still hadn't told Nicole his true relationship with Seth. At this late date, he didn't know how to broach the subject—an elephant in the room that only pinpointed his deficiencies. Their lack of communication on the subject was a direct reflection on him. He'd avoided the subject, and now it was coming back to bite him in the butt.

How in the hell was he going to live without her? Sometimes doing the right thing stank.

The box of pictures his mom had given him, all from his boyhood, weighed heavily on his lap. The photos were enough to remind him where he'd come from. He didn't fit in with Nicole. Once she saw the pictures, she'd realize that fact. Better to cut the cord now than later, when he'd be more in love with her.

Cam glanced at the heavens. Could Seth see them from above? More than likely his friend hadn't had a full-blown relationship in mind, complete with Cam sleeping with Nicole, when Seth elicited his promise. A selfish act on Cam's part. Distancing himself from her was the only solution. Thankfully, Cam's full schedule during the next few weeks would make the task easier.

Chapter 18

Nicole bent down on one knee to help slip Bobby Westerfield's backpack onto his shoulders. "Have a good weekend." The bus would be here any minute.

"Thanks, Miss Murphy." Bobby grinned. "I told my mom I'm going to marry someone just like you." He gave her a quick hug before hightailing it toward the school's entrance.

Nicole stood and watched him blend in with a dozen others scampering out the door with purpose. Her smile broadened of its own accord. Being with the kids was a rush like no other. How had she spent the last year away from doing something she loved?

Well, no more, she thought, heading back into her classroom to gather her purse and laptop. On her way out, she straightened a few desks and a note fell out of one. She picked it up off the floor and opened it.

Thanks for giving DeShawn extra attention in class. He's a good boy and he needs it, was scribbled in pencil. She folded the paper and stuck it in her pocket, glad she'd taken the time to ensure DeShawn and Timmy, another boy in her class whose clothes were worn and ill-fitting, felt welcome. The painful experiences Cam had mentioned had struck a nerve with Nicole. Her goal was to do everything in her power to continue paying special attention to those who needed it most.

On the way to her car, her cell phone rang. Nicole hurriedly opened the car door, threw her stuff on the passenger seat, and climbed inside. After noting Mary Ann's name on the caller ID, she grinned. "Hi. What's up?"

"I just called to see how things are going with you and Cam," her sister said.

"Great," Nicole replied, even though she hadn't seen the man in over a week.

"How about you two joining us for dinner tonight?"

"We can't. He's volunteering at the rehab center until ten." What Nicole didn't add was that he had nixed her suggestion to get together afterward, claiming he'd probably be too tired. Instead, she said, "What about tomorrow night?"

That would give her a good reason to swing by the rehab center and pay a visit. She'd been meaning to anyway. At least now her visit wouldn't blatantly showcase her insecurities about Cam's absence during the last eight days. Of course his schedule was crazy busy, but Nicole couldn't help thinking there might be some underlying reason other than work keeping him away. Lord, she hoped not.

Nicole sped home, and after doing a quick change, was on the way to the center before she lost her nerve.

The place looked just as she'd pictured in her mind. A two-story brick structure and plenty of parking in front. She pulled into one of the empty spaces, shifted into park, and had to inhale a few times to ease the sudden crop of butterflies now flapping inside her tummy.

It was silly to be nervous. *Just go for it.*

Inhaling another deep breath and wiping her sweaty palms on her jeans, she shoved the car door open and stepped out.

She stopped at the front desk and smiled at the gentleman behind it. "I'm here to see Cam. He promised me a tour. Do you know where he's working?"

"You mean Roberto Camareno?"

Nicole nodded. "Yes."

"He was here last night, ma'am." The man clicked his mouse and glanced at the computer screen in front of him. "I don't think he's coming in tonight. At least, he's not on the schedule."

Furrowing her brow, she attempted to keep the surprise out of her voice. "Really?"

Why had Cam told her differently? Maybe he was coming in on his own and just hadn't shown up yet. That made sense. Although she had the disconcerting notion that he was dodging her. Unfortunately, the only way that made sense—

A bouncing noise drew her out of her troubling thoughts, and she spun around.

A black man walked up to her so gracefully, she'd have never known he was missing one of his legs below the knee if he hadn't been wearing shorts. "You must be Nicole Murphy," he said as he dribbled a basketball.

"Yes, I am." She gave a brief nod and met his interested gaze. "But I'm afraid you have me at a disadvantage. I don't know your name."

His rich laugh ended in a huge smile, complete with dimples. "Easy to rectify. Tahoe King at your service." He held out a hand. "Don't worry. I'm not a stalker, I promise."

Nicole laughed and shook her head. "I wasn't worried, just curious."

"I was in Seth's unit and recognized your picture. He used to talk about you all the time." A solemn expression took over his features. "I'm sorry for your loss. I wanted to attend his memorial, but I was laid up at the time." He lifted his leg, patted the blade, and added, "You understand, I hope?"

"Of course." She cleared her throat and tucked her hair behind one ear. "I just stopped by to see Cam, who promised to show me around, but apparently I got my days mixed up. I'll see myself out."

"Well, hey, since you're already here, why don't you let me give you the fifty-cent tour? Even better, I'll only charge you a quarter. A pretty face always perks up the guys and makes them work harder."

"Okay. I'd like that." She followed him through a couple of double doors, the last pair opening to an indoor court.

"They're playing basketball in here," Tahoe explained.

"Are you sure we're not interrupting anything?"

Tahoe shook his head. "No. They get so engrossed in the game, they won't even know we're here."

Ten guys in wheelchairs were spread out along the hardwood floor. How they all maneuvered the ball while dribbling and wheeling toward the basket was beyond her, but they moved just as fast as if they'd been running. Fascinated, she leaned against the wall and watched. Every man had full control of where he was going, and if he happened to have the ball, his main goal was to shoot. More attempts than not were successful.

Eventually the game ended, and the men who'd been engrossed in playing finally noticed them and began wheeling in their direction.

Grinning, Tahoe nodded. "I'm sure they're dying to meet you. Come on and I'll introduce you."

Nicole followed his lead. A few in the chairs had prosthetic legs. One had a prosthetic arm. Most wore no prosthetic at all.

She shook hands, having a hard time remembering so many names.

A whistle blew, and their little meet-and-greet session came to a quick end as the men wheeled toward the double doors, disappearing one by one.

Tahoe turned to her. "They now have individualized therapy. Mainly that consists of weight training and walking, or learning to walk, then massages afterward to work the kinks out."

"The way some of them handled the ball, it was as if they weren't handicapped at all." To watch them play, it certainly seemed that way.

"That's the facility's aim. Loss of a limb only limits a person who lets it become a handicap." He started back out the way they'd come. "Now two or more limbs? That's where it gets challenging. As long as a person still has mental capacity, he or she can learn to function, given the right training."

"Amazing," Nicole whispered, at a loss for another word to describe what she was learning.

"You know, Cam and I were in Seth's unit on the day he died." Tahoe patted his thigh. "It's how I got this injury. I'm glad to see Cam looked you up, considering the promise he made to Seth right before he died."

"What?" Nicole halted and grabbed his arm to stop him. When he turned to face her, she asked, "You were there when Seth died? Along with Cam?" Of course, she figured Cam knew Seth; she just hadn't known they were in the same accident.

"Yes, ma'am. Worst day of my life. I still have nightmares about the kid who tossed the IED under the truck. He probably had no clue of the carnage he caused. Hell, for that matter, no one filled him in on the fact that he'd die for the deed." He ground his teeth together and scowled. "Fuckin' terrorists. They use ignorance as a means of exploitation. And they're good at it."

"Tell me about that day." She glanced down at his leg and then back up at his face. "Unless it's too painful to talk about."

"Hell no, it ain't too painful." He wiped at his face and his grin was back. "Talking about it makes it easier to bear." He squinted, eyeing her curiously. "But I'm wondering why Cam didn't tell you, seeing as he was the medic in charge when the truck exploded. In fact, Seth died in his arms on the way to the field hospital."

Cam was with Seth when he died? Nicole struggled to keep the shock off her face. Pain she hadn't felt in weeks engulfed her, only this pain was harsher because it was the pain of betrayal. He knew how important it was for her to learn about how Seth died, and he'd completely disregarded her feelings.

Somehow she got through the next fifteen minutes, holding a frozen smile on her lips while listening to Tahoe give a full rendition of that day. Thank God she didn't have to speak afterward either, as the men Tahoe introduced seemed happy to do all the talking.

"Is everything okay?" Tahoe asked the question once the double doors of the therapy section closed behind them and they were out of everyone's earshot.

No, she was not okay. She managed a nod and murmured, "I'm fine. Just tired." By this point she was seething and raring to go a few rounds, if only to assuage some of the pangs piercing her heart.

Thankfully, they made it to the facility's main entrance.

Tahoe stopped. "Well, that's it for the tour. Feel free to come back anytime. We can always use a good volunteer."

In a hurry to make it to her car before she fell apart, Nicole offered the best smile she could muster under the circumstances. "I plan to. Thanks for everything."

134

She then turned and walked briskly through the double doors that opened automatically. The second they closed, she finally let the tears fall.

Chapter 19

A loud banging on his door pulled Cam out of his thoughts as he sat staring at the electric fireplace's fake flames. In three quick steps, he was able to peek through the peephole. He struggled to suppress his shock at finding Nicole in front of him after opening the door.

He had to clench his hands into fists to keep from pulling her into a hug.

"Well?" His whispered voice cut into the silence once his shock wore off. Now was not the time to back down on his resolve to break things off with her. "Are you going to tell me why you're here?"

A spark of anger hit her eyes and as she stepped inside, the look morphed into a glare that could make an Eskimo shiver.

Again, no one spoke until Cam said, "You've obviously got something on your mind, so let's hear it. I'm not a mind reader."

"I have a strong urge to slug you, but I'll refrain. At least until I hear your side of things."

He shook his head and narrowed his gaze. "I still don't understand."

Nicole stomped her foot. Her eyes flashed accusation. "You lied to me."

He drew his brows together in confusion. "How?"

"You told me you were working at the rehab center tonight."

A streak of heat hit his cheeks. "You were at the center?" He had no reason to feel guilty when they'd not made plans.

"Damn right I was. I stopped by to see if you wanted to go to dinner with my sister and her husband tomorrow night. Silly me, I decided to ask in person, so you wouldn't be able to find another excuse to avoid me. And guess who wasn't there?"

"I got my days mixed up," Cam said. It was a blatant lie. Why couldn't he just tell her the truth and let her down gently? Because she'd wave his concerns away like the selfless person she was. He had to stay the course. "I haven't been avoiding you. I just needed a break. Things were getting too serious."

"And just when did you come to that conclusion, before or after we made love?"

The hurt in her voice was almost his undoing, but he couldn't back down now. "It was a mistake on my part."

"A mistake?" Her brown gaze studied him as a wealth of emotion crossed her face, the strongest one anguish. "Why'd you lie about the other?"

"What other?"

"You knew Seth. You were in his unit."

"I've never made a secret of that."

"You downplayed your association with him." Her voice went up a notch at the end.

"How is that lying?" He spoke in a modulated tone to calm her rising agitation.

"Omission is just another form of twisting the truth."

Cam crossed his arms and leaned a shoulder against the wall. "And what truth would that be?" He knew he was now coming across a bit too callously, but at this point he was losing the battle not to take her into his arms and tell her how much she meant to him.

"You were with Seth on the day he died."

That knocked the wind out of his verbal sails. All he was able to do was stare at her like she had ten heads.

Moisture rimmed Nicole's eyes. She blinked to clear it, but all that did was elicit more as a tear broke free. Wiping it away with one hand, she jabbed at his belly with the other. "You knew how much I wanted to know what happened on that day, and you blatantly disregarded my feelings."

How in the hell had she found out? But just as quick as the thought was out, so was another. It didn't matter. What mattered more was easing the pain etched into her features as he softened his expression. "Would it bring Seth back?"

She sniffled. "No, but at least I could put some closure on it."

"I thought you already had." He looked down to study his jeans and picked an imaginary piece of lint off of them. Then he threw out a laugh containing little humor as a new realization hit. "I should have known. I was some kind of substitute for the golden boy, wasn't I?" Pain burst in his heart, giving him the impetus to continue pushing her away.

Nicole had the gall to act affronted. "No, that's not how it is."

Cam lifted one brow. "Isn't it?"

Her eyes got rounder as if he'd actually shocked her. "You're trying to twist this around and make it my fault. I loved Seth, and I had a right to know. You had no business keeping the news from me."

"Hell if I didn't. You were so broken up over his death that your mother was afraid you'd never smile again."

"Did you promise Seth you'd look after me?"

"Yes."

"Was that the only reason you went out with me? And slept with me?"

He held up a hand, palm up. "Whoa, we're getting off track here. I admit it was a mistake to make love with you. I'm sorry for that. As for the other? If I'd have told you of my real reason for looking you up, I'd have lost you. But I never had you to begin with, did I? So, what difference would it have made?"

He turned to open the door. "I think it'll be better for both of us if you just leave."

"You're right." She looked him straight in the eyes. "I never took you for a coward. Obviously, I was wrong. I don't know what I ever saw in you. And you're wrong about being a substitute for Seth. You wouldn't be fit to shine his shoes."

The words were like a knife to his heart, cutting it to shreds as she spun around. "Good-bye, Cam. It's been nice knowing you."

If he had any doubts about his breaking things off, her look of disdain along with her sarcastic tone of voice disabused him of them. He only wished he'd done it sooner.

Yet the minute she was gone, completely out of his life for good, loneliness and heartache enveloped him. He stared at the closed door for a long while, wondering why the pain inside his gut felt like it would explode at any moment. With a heavy heart, he headed back to his chair to resume his mindless gazing into the fake electric flames.

Nicole was better off without him, so Cam had best get used to the feeling.

Chapter 20

The next week went by so slowly for Nicole that by Friday, it seemed as if a month had elapsed.

When school finally let out, she was in no hurry to make the trip to her mom and dad's house to celebrate her sister's birthday, something she had already promised to attend. After quickly navigating the empty surface streets, she veered onto the freeway entrance.

Traffic was at a standstill.

Nicole inched along, glad for the extra time to stew over her situation. It was bad enough to have to make excuses to her family about her and Cam, but when Mary Ann had called to plan another get-together, Nicole couldn't admit that her world had crumbled yet again.

Sometimes being the baby of the family stank. Everyone, especially Mary Ann, tried to solve Nicole's problems for her. It had always been that way, and usually it was easier for Nicole to just go along. Unfortunately, no one could fix this but her, so she'd pretended everything was great between them—that Cam was just super busy with school, work, and volunteering. After providing the lie, she'd suggested a weeknight date, knowing Mary Ann wouldn't go for it. At least the lie provided a bit more time to figure out things on her own.

Traffic eventually picked up, and she drove the final distance wondering how she'd get through the first five minutes without them all guessing something was wrong. To make matters worse, it was Valentine's Day. Everyone expected Cam to be with her and because he wasn't, the barrage of questions would begin.

"Hi," she shouted after opening the door and stepping inside. "I'm here." Nicole shifted out of her jacket and set it along with her gift and card for her sister on the coffee table.

Her mom came out of the kitchen. "Oh, sweetie, it's so good to see you." She looked past her shoulder toward the front door. "Where's Cam?"

"He had to work. But he sent his warm wishes." It wasn't a total lie. How she got the information out in such a matter-of-fact tone or without breaking into tears surprised her. Maybe she could do this after all. Sing happy birthday, eat, and run. Nicole smiled as she followed her mother into the dining room. "So, where is everyone?"

"They're out getting ice cream." Colleen nodded at the heart-shaped birthday cake in the center of the table. "Can't have one without the other."

Nicole remained silent as her mother went about setting out plates and forks.

"You want to tell me about it?" Colleen put down the ice cream scoop and looked at her.

Pushing a lock of hair behind one ear, Nicole cleared her throat. "About what?"

"You and Cam. What happened?"

"Why do you think something happened?"

"Oh, honey," her mother said in a soothing tone. "It's written all over your face." She pulled out two chairs, sat in one, and patted the other. "Come and tell me all about it."

Unable to stop the tears, Nicole did as requested, and the entire story came gushing out. She ended her spiel with, "Oh, Mom, he lied to me and then when I confronted him, we fought and now we're no longer together." She sniffed and wiped tears off her face. "We each said horrible things to each other. I should hate him, but truthfully, I miss him."

"I thought I raised you better than that."

"What?" Nicole wasn't after sympathy, but she certainly expected a little understanding rather than a scolding.

"Your expectations may be a little off. In fact, it seems like both of you are depending a little too heavily on the other to heal your wounds." When Nicole was about to deny this, Colleen put up a hand. "I understand your reasons for being upset, but sometimes love isn't fifty-fifty. Cam may need more understanding right now. His wounds are mental, more than likely guilt induced. He survived and Seth is dead."

Colleen looked her directly in the eyes and said, "That's a big hurdle to overcome. And who knows about his childhood?" She shrugged. "He's definitely got some baggage to get rid of. If you really loved him, you'd help him at least understand his motives. In return, I think he'll respond accordingly. That is, if he really loves you."

Her back went rigid. "How can I tell if he really loves me when he lied to me? Above all else, I need honesty."

"Then pay attention to his actions, not his words." Colleen grabbed her hands and squeezed. "Do you love him?"

"Yes. Of course I do. Otherwise I wouldn't be so upset."

"Then it's worth giving it a second chance. Love requires total commitment, even when the other person disappoints, at which point it needs forgiveness. Communication is also important. And lastly, it requires sacrificing pride when you falter."

"What if I can't do all of that?" Cam had disappointed her, and her pride had suffered because of it.

"Then maybe you're not ready. And maybe he isn't either. You're not on any deadline. True love waits. Just remember, we all deserve to be loved, especially people like Cam who don't think they are lovable."

Nicole sat there absorbing her mother's wisdom. Finally, she stood. "I need to think more about what you said." She reached for her coat and said over her shoulder on the way to the door, "Tell Caryn happy birthday."

• • •

Thank God his shift was over for the week. Cam slammed his locker shut with more force than necessary in an effort to stave off his foul mood.

"What the hell is wrong with you lately?" Scotty said, coming up behind Cam and causing him to turn around. For a long moment, he studied Cam's face as if it were a road map before he shook his head. "If I didn't know better, I'd say you've got woman troubles, except you of all people have that sewn up."

Yeah, he'd sewn that up real good. Cam looked down and studied the cracks in the concrete. Scotty didn't need to know the messed-up facts about his personal life. "You're right. I just have a lot on my mind with my mom moving in with her boyfriend."

Scotty clapped him on the back. "I hear ya. I don't know what I'd do if my mom was dating some gigolo." Then he grinned. "My dad might have some issues with it too."

Cam smiled. Not a big smile, but at least it was something. He really didn't have any issues with Anthony. Not after seeing where he lived and how well he was taking care of his mother. Still, Cam felt left out. "I gotta go and see my mom today, so thanks for the pep talk."

Rain threatened. He exited the fire station, and buttoning his jacket to ward off the cold, headed for BART. The temperature was dropping with every step, making him wish he'd already bought a car. It was at the top of his to-do list, now that he had the cash flow. He just needed to find the time to go car shopping.

Thankfully, Anthony's high-rise condominium was only a few blocks from the BART station.

"How are you today, Mr. Camareno," the doorman said after Cam pushed through the double doors of the marble-and-glass front entrance.

The opulence always made him feel a little strange, especially after being in Afghanistan and seeing how so many there lived in poverty—real poverty—where food and shelter, along with running water or electricity, weren't always available.

"Hi, George. I'm here to see my mother."

"She stepped out for her weekly massage and is due to return any moment. But Mr. Morales is in." He nodded toward the elevator. "Go on up. I'll let Mr. M know you're coming."

"Thanks." Debating his options, Cam begrudgingly punched the UP button. Meeting Anthony Morales without his mom's presence went along the same lines as cleaning the oven at the station. Necessary, but not particularly fun. Still, as he stepped into the elevator that would take him to the penthouse, he sent up a silent prayer of thanks that his mom had found someone who spared no expense in seeing to her needs. Massages helped her joints, but were a luxury Cam couldn't afford.

When the doors opened onto the spacious top-floor condo, Anthony greeted him, a genuine smile on his face. "Welcome, Cam. What brings you here?"

Cam shrugged. "I don't know," he said honestly. His entire life was different now, and he felt like a fish out of water. "I guess I just needed some company."

"Well, sit. I'd pour you a bourbon, but I know you don't drink." He started for his wet bar at the far end of the room. "How about water?"

"Water's great. Thanks." Cam ambled toward the wall of windows with a great view of San Francisco Bay. The sun had disappeared in the west, on the other side of the building, but the purples and dark blues it left were spectacular. The colors also brought out a sense of loneliness. Without someone to share such beauty, how could he feel anything else?

"You look like you lost your best friend."

Funny, that was exactly how he'd describe the sensation. "I was in the neighborhood and thought I'd stop by."

"Conchetta will be happy to see you." He handed him the bottled water. "Why don't you stay for dinner? I'll have Maria, my housekeeper, set up another plate."

"That sounds great. Thanks."

"Where is that nice young lady who helped us move your mother in here?"

"Home, most likely."

Anthony's gaze narrowed into a squint, and Cam felt like a bug under a microscope. He certainly hoped that Anthony couldn't see past his defenses. "It's Valentine's Day. You two should be together."

"We're not." Cam exhaled heavily and moved to sit on the plushest sofa he'd ever seen. Yep. His mom was definitely in a better place. She had a wait staff and chauffeur at her beck and call. And during Cam's few visits, Anthony appeared to be devoted to her, which totally eased his mind. In fact, if he hadn't been so down, he might find the situation funny in an ironic sort of way.

"Care to talk about it?" Anthony's deep voice interrupted his thoughts.

"No." Cam snorted. "It's too complicated."

Anthony sat across from him and crossed his legs. "Then, how about I talk and you listen?"

Cam rolled his eyes, not too keen on having to hear what anyone had to say on the subject of Nicole.

The older man leaned back, resting an arm on top of the cushions. "Your mother and I have had quite a few conversations about you and your father."

Cam stiffened. "Oh?" His dad was another one of those topics he'd rather avoid. "I'm not sure if that's a good thing or not." He hadn't meant to verbalize the last sentence, but since he had, he asked, "Like what?"

"I know about your dad and his weaknesses. I know about your fears of becoming like him."

"Did my mom—"

"No. Conchetta didn't have to tell me that," Anthony said, cutting him off. "That's my own take on it, based on what I felt toward my father. He was a drunk too. And his reasons weren't near as understandable as your father's. My papa just loved alcohol more than he loved himself or anyone around him." He took a sip of his bourbon, then sighed and held up the glass. "I like a glass of fine bourbon now and then, the same as a good red wine. That doesn't mean I'll turn out like my father, a man I detested."

Anthony stood, moved to the windows, and spent a few seconds peering out the glass before turning back to him. "I made a decision early on to never be like him, but in doing so I almost missed out on the best part of the last thirty years with my late wife. She was a class above me, and I didn't feel worthy enough for her." He glanced at Cam and smiled. "I could say the same about Conchetta."

"You think my mom is above you?" At first Cam had thought so, but it surprised him that Anthony, someone who had

SANDY LOYD

wealth and power, would too.

Anthony only grunted and took another swallow of bourbon. He talked of his poverty-stricken youth. They had a lot in common, especially when Anthony revealed that his dad had died of an alcohol-related incident.

"How old were you when your dad died?" Cam definitely hadn't expected to feel a connection with the guy, but that was the only way he could describe it.

"I was seventeen and already out on my own. I helped support my mother and two sisters until my mother remarried and my sisters graduated from college."

"I wish I'd had a few siblings," Cam said in a low tone, opening up a little about his lonely childhood spent with a dad who continually disappointed him.

Somehow it was easier telling Anthony what was in his heart about his alcoholic father because of their shared experiences. "I didn't have any family other than my mother to support," he said, even going so far as to admit to his unruly behavior as a teen. "I was the cause of my mother's disabilities—"

"Don't." Anthony held up a hand, stopping him cold. "You were a child . . . in despair." Anthony leaned closer. "It is the parents' duty to protect their children. Your mother knew she had failed in that respect. Your father was her choice—not yours. Your actions were attributed to his failure. Quit feeling guilty for being a rowdy *boy* who lashed out."

That made sense, but . . . "It's not that easy."

"What about how it affects your mother? By holding on to the past, you're causing her to feel just as guilty. Your youth is done. Your mistakes cannot be undone. The only way to move forward is to let it go and learn from it, which I think you have accomplished."

"I don't think I have." Cam told him about Seth, his death, his promise concerning Nicole, and all that had happened in the past two months. "Maybe I can dump my childhood guilt, but not the other guilt I feel over surviving. I especially don't feel worthy of her."

"But you *do* love her?"

146

Cam nodded. "Yes. That's why I decided to stay away." He trailed a drop of condensation on the water bottle with a finger, paying an inordinate amount of attention to his hand.

"Does she feel the same way?"

He thought about the question for a moment. "She never told me in so many words, but . . ."

Anthony smiled. "You felt her love, am I right?"

Again, Cam nodded. "Yes. I felt everything with her."

Anthony came to stand in front of him, drawing his attention. "Then you need to let her know and let her make the decision." He held Cam's gaze until Cam looked away. "Unless you're a coward, using your friend's death as a shield." Anthony shook his head. "Yet you've never given me cause to believe that about you."

The older man placed a hand on his shoulder and gave a gentle squeeze. "Take a chance, Cam. Give your heart to Nicole. Let her help with your guilt. You should be talking to her, not me."

Just then the elevator door opened, and his mother stepped out with the aid of Anthony's chauffeur.

When Conchetta noticed him, her entire being lit up. "Cam! What a nice surprise."

Cam stood and strode toward her, renewed hope for the future filling him with energy. "I came by to say hi, but now I have to go."

Confusion flashed in her eyes. "You just got here."

He laughed and bent to kiss her cheek. "I know, but today is Valentine's Day, and I have to find mine."

SANDY LOYD

Chapter 21

"Of all the days for it to snow," Nicole murmured, slowing again in the stop-and-go traffic on I-880. The white fluff fluttering about was definitely a once-in-a-lifetime occurrence around these parts. In fact, she'd never seen snowfall this far west of the Sierras. Thank God it wasn't sticking.

A car stopped suddenly in front of her, and Nicole braked. Her car skidded a bit before finally stopping a good foot from the other bumper. She took a deep breath to still her racing heart.

Darn. The roads were slick, so even if traffic started moving again, her trip would take much longer than she'd anticipated. Bay Area drivers might not have problems with rainstorms, but snow? Too many passed her like they were going to a fire. Nicole preferred to get there alive and without incident. Hopefully tonight.

What if Cam weren't there? What if he was working or at the rehab center? She should have called first. These and more thoughts like them streamed through her mind as she eased forward twenty feet. Somehow she'd found the courage to drop everything to visit him and tell him what was in her heart. Only now she started questioning her reasoning. Especially with the white stuff coming down.

What if he thought she was stalking him?

That brought out an urge to smile. Heavens, she had to resort to stalking to catch him off guard. Otherwise she sensed he'd put up a shield, and then she'd have to wait longer.

It was Valentine's Day and by its very meaning, was a day for love to flourish. Her mom had been wrong when she'd indicated that maybe Nicole wasn't ready. She was ready. What made her believe so strongly in the notion was her willingness to wait until

Cam was ready. Letting him in on what lay in her heart was something she wasn't willing to wait on.

All it took to reach that conclusion was for her to remember Cam's promise about waiting on Christmas Eve. It seemed like such a long time ago. Yet nearly two months had passed, and in that time, a lot had happened.

Eventually traffic snaked by the cause of the delay, an accident. Obviously one of those fire chasers had run into a car when it lost control while trying to stop. Thankfully, it only looked like a fender bender.

Filled with resolve, Nicole kept up a steady speed as she drove the rest of the way to Cam's apartment. Forty minutes later, she pulled into the parking lot. By now the snow was sticking on the grass and the trees. Two palm trees, one on each side of the entrance, caught her attention. It seemed odd to see snow on the fronds. Laughing, Nicole stepped out of the car and reached for her cell phone to capture the moment.

As more snow fell, silence surrounded her, providing an eerie quality to the night, something she'd probably never see again in her lifetime.

Absorbed in taking the shot, she hadn't realized she had company in the quiet lot until she felt hands on her waist.

About to scream, she swung around, keys curled inside fingers ready to strike the guy's nose. Her hand halted in midair. She recognized Cam just as he yelled, "I give up. Don't hurt me!"

Nicole lowered her arm. "Cam?"

"Yeah, it's me. What're you doing here?"

She swallowed hard. Lord above, now was not the time to back down on her mission, but after staring into his guarded gaze, her resolve wavered a bit. Clearing her throat, she rocked back on her heels.

She was saved from having to answer when he held his arms out in a wide welcome.

"Doesn't matter," he said. "I'm just glad you're here."

Grinning, she stepped closer, reached up on tippy-toes, and kissed him. His arms went around her, and though it was still snowing, warmth surrounded her as his lips softened. How she loved this man. He wasn't a substitute. Cam was the real thing.

He broke the kiss, then grabbed her hand. "Come on, you're getting drenched out here."

If she had any doubts about timing, the smoldering look he sent her disavowed her of them.

Laughing, she dusted the snow off her shoulders and followed him inside.

Once they made it to his apartment, Cam let the door slam behind him. "Now, where were we?"

"I believe we were about to make love," she said, wrapping her hands around his neck and pulling his head closer.

He nipped her lips. His mouth found its way to her ear, where he spent a moment nibbling. "I believe you're right." He then picked her up as if she weighed nothing and carried her through the hallway toward his bedroom.

Another laugh rose up as he dropped unceremoniously on the bed. Her laugh turned into a quiet moan when his lips covered hers.

Like all the other times they'd made love, Cam did so slowly, drawing out her emotion a kiss or a touch at a time. Her body came alive under his touch. How she'd missed him this past week.

"I love you," she said into his mouth as he entered her. "My heart is free and it chooses you."

Then everything but Cam faded. Just before she found her release, he rose up and caught her gaze. The intensity of it as they went off the cliff together would be etched in her memory forever. There was no denying the love in those soulful brown eyes.

• • •

Cam spent a long while floating back to earth after their lovemaking. Finally, he lifted off Nicole and situated her next to him, with her head cradled within the curve of his upper arm.

"I'm sorry for the horrible things I said and the horrible way I treated you." As he spoke, his hand trailed up and down her arm. Nicole had the softest skin, and he doubted he'd ever tire of touching her. "You of all people didn't deserve it."

"I spoke out of line too. I'm sorry for hurting you," she whispered. "I thought you had only used me, and then . . ." Her voice broke with emotion.

Cam kissed the top of her forehead. "Never." He planted another kiss, this time on her cheek. "I know I'll never be able to take Seth's—"

Her finger stopped him from finishing his sentence. "You're not a substitute. You're someone I love." Nicole sat up and leaned over so he could glimpse into her eyes. "I can't pretend I didn't love Seth too. All I can say is that my heart has plenty of room for you. I love you. And that's a good thing, when at one time I thought I would never be able to say those words again."

The honesty gleaming from her gaze nearly felled him as did her declaration of love. For the first time in his life, the promise of tomorrow was staring him straight in the face.

Cam would be a fool not to grab onto it and never let go. "I love you," he whispered, capturing her lips.

Epilogue

"I can't believe I let you drag me here." Cam exhaled a long breath and stared out at the church parking lot Nicole had just pulled into.

"What?" She shifted into park and unclipped her belt. "You'll have a great time." Nicole jumped out.

Cam slowly followed. "I'm not into bingo." Even if Anthony and Conchetta were joining them. He let the car door slam behind him and caught up with her as she clicked the automatic locks. For the hundredth time, he tried to tell her that he didn't like crowds. Especially if the crowds consisted of churchgoers.

"You can do this," Nicole said, reaching out and weaving her fingers through his. "You're not that needy, gangly kid any longer." She squeezed his hand to reinforce the statement. "You're a contributing member of society, so you should darn well get over your phobias."

"That's what I get for confiding in you," he said under his breath.

"I caught that. Suck it up, Cam." She smiled. "You'll be fine."

Cam muttered an oath. It didn't help that she was right.

The room was packed with what Nicole termed "diehard bingo players." No one took any notice of them as they made their way to a table in the back of the room, too busy situating their playing cards and gossiping.

Colleen and Maggie saw them and waved cheerfully.

"So glad you could make it," Colleen said as Nicole pulled out a chair.

Introductions went back and forth.

Between the two older ladies and Nicole, Cam had met tons of new people. Keeping track was useless. Cam waved hello, kissed his mom on the cheek, shook Anthony's hand, and sat next to his fiancée.

The word elicited an urge to grin. *Imagine*! He was getting married.

He glanced up just in time to catch Colleen's assessing gaze. She then turned to Maggie and said, "Two down and seven more to go."

If he didn't know better, he'd think she was gloating. Then, when Maggie held up a hand and Colleen high-fived her, he laughed. "You guys are good."

He picked up the stack of cards in front of him, almost feeling sorry for Nicole's siblings. Cam glanced at Nicole and smiled. Almost, but not quite, considering the love he'd found. Thanks to Colleen and Maggie, he'd found his promise of tomorrow, and he couldn't wait for tomorrow to come.

~~~*THE END*~~~

Author's Note

Thanks for reading *The Promise of Tomorrow*, (book five in The California Series). I hope you enjoyed it!

If you'd like to read more of the series, two three-book bundles are available:

California Series – Books 1, 2, & 3: Three couples find their way to love and happiness in these first three heartwarming stories all set in the San Francisco Bay area. Cozy up to the fire and fall in love with *Winter Interlude*. Experience a flirty, sexy, and fun romance on a San Francisco night in *Promises, Promises*. And read about *James*, a man women love who has one flaw—he can't commit.

California Series – Books 2, 3, & 4: This set is for readers who have already read *Winter Interlude*. It includes *Promises, Promises* as well as *James* and *Dancing With an Angel*.

If you'd like to know when my next book in the series is available, simply sign up for my newsletter on my website www.sandyloyd.com or e-mail me at sandyloyd@twc.com, and I'll add you to my list.

Please consider reviewing this book. Reviews help other readers find books. I appreciate all reviews, whether positive or negative.

Follow me on Twitter at @sloydwrites, or like my Facebook page at facebook.com/sloydwrites.

About The Author

Sandy Loyd is a Western girl through and through. Born and raised in Salt Lake City, she's worked and lived in some fabulous places in the US including Arizona, Northern California, and South Florida. An empty nester with almost two dozen books published, she now resides in Kentucky and writes full time. As much as she loves her current hometown, she misses the mountains and has to go back to her roots to get her mountain fix at least once a year; otherwise, her muse suffers.

She spent her single years in San Francisco and considers that city one of America's treasures, comparable to no other city in the world. Her California Series, starting out with *Winter Interlude*, are all set in the Bay Area. Her series consists of fun, heartwarming stories about crazy friends who, like single people everywhere, are seeking that someone special to share their lives with among thousands of eligible candidates.

Sandy's first published romantic-suspense novel, *The Sin Factor*, set in another wonderful US city, Washington, DC, was the first book in the DC Badboys Series. *Raising the Stakes* is book two.

She has since published two more romantic-suspense novels set in fictional towns in Kentucky to give a reader a feel for small-town living. *Running From Love*'s setting showcases the state's caves and lakes.

Sandy believes the United States is immensely diverse, and her experiences have provided much fodder to write about. She spent a decade in South Florida diving, sailing, and enjoying other activities on the water. *Tropical Spice* is set in the Florida Keys. If you'd like to read more of her work, an excerpt of *Tropical Spice* is provided below.

Excerpt: Tropical Spice

In this fun, flirty beach read, Pepper Grady is in charge of her own destiny—one that doesn't include being ruled by an overbearing man like her father. She vows that she will never accept marriage to a man who can't remain faithful. Yet when she meets a hunky Latino dynamo, she allows herself to indulge in a romantic fling—since an arrogant alpha male has no place in her new life.

Ñico Guerrero doesn't believe in love. But in order to please his dying father, he travels to Grassy Key to convince his runaway betrothed to return with him to Isla de Diablo, where he'll take her as his wife. When he realizes he's been seduced by the beautiful heiress, he has to make a choice. After all, passion fades and he is his father's son, so he's not sure he can promise what she desperately wants . . . a lifetime of love and fidelity.

CHAPTER 1

Hunks who stepped over Second Chances' threshold normally didn't interest Pepper Grady. Not when the steady stream of hot-looking guys searching for a way to wind down after a day on the water never ended. Something about this one, as he strode through the bar with confidence evident in every step, drew her surreptitious gaze. A ray of light framed his face and highlighted strong aquiline features better than a Sharpie. And even more interesting? Every woman in the place noticed him. He was well aware of it. The sultry gleam emanating from those dark brown, soul-searing eyes told her so.

Okay. He was definitely worth a second glance, not to

mention lots of ogling.

Second Chances wasn't exactly a gin joint—more like an upscale tourist hangout in the Florida Keys. Despite that, Pepper, a self-proclaimed classic movie aficionado, had a better appreciation for Humphrey Bogart's point of view when Ingrid walked into his life in Casablanca. Her attention stayed glued to the hunk as he sauntered farther into the packed room even as the crowd seemed to part, allowing him space to navigate.

He gave the place a covert scan. When his focus landed her way, little tingles of awareness walked up her spine. Ignoring the sensation, Pepper sucked in a huge breath and wiped the bar in quick, easy motions in an effort to disengage from the stranger's pull.

He was only a male. One who probably expected women to bow at his feet . . . expected his charm and dynamite looks to pave the way to whatever he wanted, which Pepper figured amounted to a night in bed.

She grinned and gave the tall, well-toned mass of masculine perfection another stealthy once-over. The idea held merit. The minute the thought leaped out, Pepper discarded it. The guy looked too cocky. Besides, he had enough adulation without adding hers.

He'd clearly ranked at the top of his class in Seduction 101. No different from the thousands she'd seen in the three years she'd co-owned the bar. Of those thousands, more than half wore the same cap and gown of attitude . . . had graduated to the highest level. The stud level. All had the same moves, with all the same lines.

Pepper could recite most word for word. She'd heard them too many times. A sliver of regret slid over her at the idea that he'd be so unoriginal. How disappointing.

When he pulled out a stool not two feet away, she felt his gaze and her heartbeat quickened. The hairs on the back of her neck stood up. She didn't appreciate either reaction.

After a quick overview of the bar patrons and noting only full drinks, she turned her attention to washing glasses. Refills could wait, allowing a moment to reflect on the stranger's effect. Why did he cause such strong sensations? Was it pheromones? Some kind of magnetic attraction? Steeling herself, she glanced up, presenting her perfected bartender smile.

"What can I get you?" She was totally amazed at how calm her voice sounded despite how every nerve ending she possessed stood at full alert.

"What do you recommend?"

Mercy! Even his voice was sexy ... exuding an arrogant maleness that said he conquered all women and took no prisoners. "Depends," she shot back, reaching for normal.

"Oh?"

"Yeah." Pepper's smile broadened, becoming more genuine. "Are you in the mood for a beer or would you like to experience a bit of the Keys?" She risked a quick glance at his eyes. Wrong thing to do. She refocused on a goblet and washed it for the third time.

"I think it's clean enough."

"What?" She looked up again and froze. A generous smile had taken over his face.

Ignore that smile. He's not charming. Do not let him get to you.

Point one went to the stranger, but a point was all she'd allow in his game. She straightened her spine and concentrated on rinsing the glass. In slow motion, she placed it on the strainer, before wiping her wet hands on her apron.

Her focus lifted, meeting his amused gaze. "I think you need Second Chances' specialty."

"Oh?" He hesitated a heartbeat. "I'm more interested in your specialty."

So sad and so expected. She'd heard that phrase just once too often.

Pepper flaunted a toothy grin, taking the point. "My specialty is shooting down guys like you without hurting egos. After all, I work for tips." She plunked the drink she'd hastily prepared in front of him, increased the wattage of her smile at the same time, and winked. "That'll be six dollars. Would you like to run a tab?"

Grin fading, he eyed her intently. Suddenly, another smile

took his face, absolutely stealing her air, the punch of its effect landing with a hard thud against her chest.

"One will do." He pulled out his wallet and dropped a ten on the bar. "Keep the change. My ego is still intact."

Something in the way he said the words, a bit of Spanish inflection she hadn't heard earlier, caught her attention. Images of her father and older brother flashed through her mind. Then she rejected the notion. They had no clue as to her whereabouts. She'd hidden her past well. Angelina Delgado didn't exist in Marathon, Florida, gateway to some of the best sport fishing and scuba diving in the world. The key was miles away from the Caribbean island of her youth. Far from an overbearing padré determined to rule her life with his outdated notions. No one knew of Pepper Grady's auspicious beginnings. And she meant to keep it that way.

"Can I get another?"

She spun in the direction of the voice at the other end of the bar. "Coming right up." Pushing away thoughts of the stranger, she grabbed the lever, filled a chilled glass from the tap, then switched the full beer with the empty as she palmed the five the tourist held out.

With business brisk, she poured nonstop drinks as he slipped into the background. During a lull twenty minutes later, Pepper discreetly scanned the crowded bar noting, with not a little regret, he'd disappeared. She sighed. The stud was just another customer who tried to win her over and lost. Nothing more. Nothing less. For the rest of the night, she stayed too busy pouring drinks to worry over her reaction, much less think about it.

Eventually, the last customer finally left indicating the end of her shift. Damn, her feet hurt from standing on the bar's concrete floor for so long. Friday nights were always the busiest, meaning she usually worked from opening until closing. Thank goodness she only had one more hectic night before her vacation began. Then she'd have a week to do nothing but drive to Key West and hang out, or maybe head north to Miami for some shopping.

"Good night, Rach." Pepper nodded on her way out.

Co-owner Rachel Smith glanced up from her paperwork. "G'night."

Karen Black, the third partner and person in charge of the restaurant end of the bar, had left earlier, not long after the kitchen closed. Rachel handled details like withholding taxes and ordering because it was her strength. Pepper's was handling the customers. Their arrangement worked, affording the trio a lucrative lifestyle while living in paradise.

Pepper locked the door behind her. Rachel had a habit of working well past the one a.m. closing. Things were quiet on Grassy Key, given its location and Second Chances' high-end clientele this time of year, but why ask for trouble?

Late April meant weekends filled with South Floridians wanting a quick getaway, and vacationing hard-core divers or sport fishermen who left at the crack of dawn. All were usually ready for a drink and relaxation earlier than most vacationers, also ending their evenings earlier. Lack of sleep and too much alcohol could disrupt a diver's time underwater. And sport fishermen were more interested in their next day's catch than in being wild and crazy all night.

The minute the balmy night air hit her face, Pepper undid the scrunchie holding her thick black waist-length hair. Its heaviness fell like a mantle around her shoulders. Bending over, she rubbed her temples and pulled a hand through the lush tresses to allow the cooling effect the Atlantic Ocean's breeze provided. Long hair and tropical humidity didn't mix well, but Pepper couldn't bring herself to chop it off, dealing with its length and thickness as best she could. Someday she'd tire of having a furnace on her head. Until then, she'd persevere.

She straightened, surveyed the parking lot, and stopped abruptly, fingers still laced in her hair. Ignoring the little spark of pleasure spreading throughout her system, her elbow dropped. Then she ambled toward the dark shape perched against the hood of a sleek car, forgetting all about sore feet.

Pepper's stare remained steady, watching him watch her as she approached. His presence provided an element of excitement she hadn't felt in a long, long time, which only meant her life had become pretty damn boring. She halted a safe distance in front of him and crossed her arms. Whether a protective move or not, she wasn't sure.

"Fancy seeing you here." Her gaze took a trip over his gorgeous body, a twelve on a scale of one to ten. Though he sported the basic Keys wardrobe of shorts and a polo shirt—his were expensive and sheathed well-defined muscles like a glove.

"It's no accident," he said. "I'm waiting for you."

"Really?" She lifted her eyebrows and studied his masculine features, as she hadn't done earlier. Yep! Definitely Latin descent. The shadows magnified his dark hair and eyes. He probably lived in Miami. The slight inflection she caught again told her Spanish was his first language, most likely spoken at home. She'd heard the subtle nuances too often during her youth not to recognize his flawless English was a close second. Maybe his parents or grandparents were Cuban immigrants. Since Cuba was in the opposite direction of Isla del Diablo, she exhaled a sigh of relief.

"Yes, really." He grinned, the parking lot lights reflecting off straight white teeth. "It's huge."

When confusion clouded her eyes, a taunting midnight gaze seized and held hers.

"My ego, among other more important things," he clarified, still smiling.

She laughed, unable to hold back the burst of amusement. Point to the stranger, his taunts unexpected and refreshing. "Nice to know." Pepper turned to start off in the direction of her house, a short walk she made nightly, and said over her shoulder, "But I'm not interested in egos or other things."

Attractive or not, everything about him shouted one-night stand and she was anything but. Though, surprisingly enough, she found herself tempted, which was why she opted for retreat.

"You're walking?" The incredulity in his loud voice disrupted the night sounds. The tree frogs and crickets quieted. An eerie silence trailed in the aftermath.

She pivoted, walking backward, and nodded. "Good deduction, I'm walking." As if on cue, the chorus began anew. She spun back around and continued, half hoping he'd follow, if only to keep the game alive for a bit longer. She had to admit, he didn't bore her.

Within a moment, she felt his presence behind her. "I will escort you." The words were not a question, more like a command, nor did she miss the arrogance in them.

"Suit yourself." She shrugged, completely used to that Latino male superiority, one she'd encountered most of her life. "It's not far."

Sparing him a brief glimpse, she caught something in the firm line of his jaw.

Definitely a Hispanic male. His every ounce of masculinity conveyed the idea that she, a mere woman, couldn't manage on her own without his protection—a total misassumption.

Extensive tae kwon do training, along with the Monroe County Sheriff Department's defensive maneuvers course she'd taken after first setting foot in Florida, negated his false notion. Having been a pampered rich girl her entire life, she'd wanted to be able to defend herself in case the unthinkable happened. Single women without family nearby were easy targets. And Pepper decided long ago to be no man's easy target—even her father's—and certainly not this stranger's. She smiled inwardly. "I can take care of myself."

"A fact I have discovered firsthand."

She slanted another glance in his direction. The smug smile had returned.

Such a Spaniard! A hard one to ignore when he viewed her as if she were his next meal. Funny, how on other men that look was always enough to earn a quick put-down, but on him, it only made her wonder what would happen if . . .

"I do this for my own satisfaction. What kind of man would I be to let a beautiful woman walk the streets alone at this hour?"

What kind indeed, she thought, not replying and trying to ignore the companionable silence that had suddenly sprung up between them.

Neither spoke for nearly a quarter of a block before he asked, "Do my noble efforts gain me a name? Maybe some idle chitchat?"

Another laugh broke free. He'd earned another point. She'd best be careful, else he might win more than her name. This intriguing stranger had the uncanny ability to steal the game. She inhaled deeply, lightly biting her bottom lip, giving him a considering perusal.

"Pepper," she said, after a long moment and deciding she liked him. "Pepper Grady. Mr. . . . ?"

"Nick Guerrero." He stuck out his hand.

"It's nice to meet you, Nick." She shook hands, noting a firm grip, also noting the way a spark of energy zapped life into her fingers. She swallowed hard, fighting stimulating sensations. "And what else do you hope your gallantry accomplishes?"

"That should be easy to deduce."

By this point, both had stopped walking. His smile, along with the amusement flashing from his eyes, almost lit the night sky. Yet she noted an unexpected sincerity in that gaze that was much more seductive. She tried to pull her hand away but his hold tightened, sending her heartbeat soaring. When he took her wrist to his mouth, she steeled her pulse to slow, praying he wouldn't notice how fast it zoomed.

"My lady's favor," he murmured, kissing that most sensitive spot just above her palm.

The heated tone in his voice spread over her like a warm blanket. And she wished his mouth wasn't so caressing . . . so moist . . . so inciting. In tandem, they ignited sparks. Uncontrolled pleasure shot everywhere. She shouldn't be aroused. Not with such a lame line and a smooth move, but she had to admit, they did the trick.

Now she understood why others succumbed to the exquisite torment. One consisting of a combination of timing, attraction, pheromones, and who knew what else, that went into the perfect seduction. She darn sure didn't think conditions got more perfect than this. Pepper had never felt this free, this alive, or this needy. Not like he made her feel at the exact moment she'd finally yanked her fingers from his grasp.

Alarm bells pealed in her brain. This man was dangerous.

For the first time in Pepper's life, she could see herself in the throes of passion. With Nick. Very disturbing, given she'd just met him and knew nothing about him. Though many had tried, no man had ever wielded such influence after only a short walk and a few words.

Secretly, she observed him, searching for some clue as to why him. Why now?

In an instant of insight, the truth hit. He epitomized men of power and wealth, men she'd sworn off, men like her father and her brother. The same supreme confidence the Delgado men exuded was stamped into every nuance of his body.

Pepper stiffened. Her pulse quickened. Only this time, the cause was wariness over his nearness, not excitement.

Walk. Just keep walking. Adhering to her mental commands, she forced movement, put one foot in front of the other.

He followed, strolling silently beside her. Of course he would. He had to sense he was close to his prize. A hunting tiger aware of his tiring prey.

The closer they got to her house, the more wary she became, even regretting her impulse to allow his escort. Oh, she wasn't afraid of him in the sense that he might harm her. This fear went deeper because he'd somehow snuck in under her guard.

Looking straight ahead, her mind spun as more similarities surfaced. Oh, yes. The signs were there. Hadn't she escaped her father's heavy hand and become who she wanted to be ... her own woman? She'd come too far to let a man like Nick Guerrero waltz into her life and begin controlling.

She'd survived thus far without having passion in her life. Passion was overrated anyway, made heartbroken fools of women. Her mother's life, a prime example, was one Pepper had no intention of replicating. Ever.

Tropical Spice – Book 1

www.ingramcontent.com/pod-product-compliance
Lightning Source LLC
Chambersburg PA
CBHW020252130626
46549CB00005B/2184